Amy Cross is the author of more than 200 horror, paranormal, fantasy and thriller novels.

OTHER TITLES BY AMY CROSS INCLUDE

1689
American Coven
Annie's Room
The Ash House
Asylum
B&B
The Bride of Ashbyrn House
The Cemetery Ghost
The Curse of the Langfords
The Devil, the Witch and the Whore
Devil's Briar
The Disappearance of Lonnie James
Eli's Town
The Farm
The Ghost of Molly Holt
The Ghosts of Lakeforth Hotel
The Girl Who Never Came Back
Haunted
The Haunting of Blackwych Grange
The Haunting of Nelson Street
The House on Fisher Street
The House Where She Died
Out There
Stephen
The Shades
The Soul Auction
Trill

THE HAUNTINGS OF MIA RUSH

AMY CROSS

This edition
first published by Blackwych Books Ltd
United Kingdom, 2023

Copyright © 2023 Blackwych Books Ltd

All rights reserved. This book is a work of fiction.
Names, characters, places, incidents and businesses are
the product of the author's imagination or are
used fictitiously. Any resemblance to actual persons,
living or dead, or to actual events or locations,
is entirely coincidental.

Also available in e-book format.

www.blackwychbooks.com

CONTENTS

PROLOGUE
page 15

CHAPTER ONE
page 17

CHAPTER TWO
page 25

CHAPTER THREE
page 33

CHAPTER FOUR
page 41

CHAPTER FIVE
page 49

CHAPTER SIX
page 57

CHAPTER SEVEN
page 65

CHAPTER EIGHT
page 73

CHAPTER NINE
page 81

CHAPTER TEN
page 89

CHAPTER ELEVEN
page 97

CHAPTER TWELVE
page 105

CHAPTER THIRTEEN
page 113

CHAPTER FOURTEEN
page 121

CHAPTER FIFTEEN
page 129

CHAPTER SIXTEEN
page 137

CHAPTER SEVENTEEN
page 147

CHAPTER EIGHTEEN
page 157

CHAPTER NINETEEN
page 165

CHAPTER TWENTY
page 173

CHAPTER TWENTY-ONE
page 181

CHAPTER TWENTY-TWO
page 191

CHAPTER TWENTY-THREE
page 199

CHAPTER TWENTY-FOUR
page 207

CHAPTER TWENTY-FIVE
page 215

CHAPTER TWENTY-SIX
page 223

CHAPTER TWENTY-SEVEN
page 231

CHAPTER TWENTY-EIGHT
page 239

CHAPTER TWENTY-NINE
page 247

CHAPTER THIRTY
page 255

EPILOGUE
page 263

THE HAUNTINGS OF MIA RUSH

PROLOGUE

Holding his daughter in his arms, David stepped into the doorway and looked into the kitchen. He immediately flinched as he saw Mia standing in the middle of the room, soaked in blood.

Behind her, more blood was dribbling off the side of the table, while a body lay on the floor.

"It's okay," Mia said, her eyes glistening with tears as a smile spread across her face. Stepping forward, she reached out and took little Catherine from her husband's arms. "There's no need to be scared. Mummy's here now."

CHAPTER ONE

One month earlier...

SITTING ON THE STEPS leading up to the back porch, Mia Rush looked out at the garden and watched as a gentle breeze blew across the grass.

"Hey," her husband David said, stepping out from the house and making his way down to join her. "*There* are my two favorite girls in all the whole world. I've been searching for you two lovely ladies everywhere."

Stopping next to the pram, he looked down and saw two-week-old Catherine sleeping happily under a beautiful knitted white blanket. He reached down and touched one of her hands, and the baby merely gurgled happily as she continued to rest.

After taking a moment to make sure the blanket was properly tucked, David adjusted the sun-guard that kept Catherine in the shade.

"I just realized something weird," Mia said.

David turned to her.

"I realized that this is perfect," Mia continued. "This whole situation. Moving here, I mean, to the countryside, with Catherine and with you. I've got my work figured out, and you've got your job set up so you can do most of it remotely, and we both love what we do. I know how crazy this is going to sound, and probably a little insufferable, but I've just realized that I don't have anything to worry about. Nothing! I don't have a care in the world! Everything I always dreamed of has finally come true." She paused, as if she truly couldn't quite believe what she was about to say. "My life is literally perfect."

"Mine too," David said with a smile.

"It won't last, of course," she countered.

"Says who?"

"Says reality," she pointed out with a smile. "I know that life just doesn't work that way, but I wanted to take a moment to be thankful for the way things have developed. That last round of treatment was such a long-shot, yet somehow the embryo took and despite all the odds Catherine's a happy, healthy baby. She's a miracle, if you think about it. *Everything* in our lives right now is a miracle. I guess that's what I was trying to get at just now. This is the most perfect moment I could ever possibly imagine. In fact, I'm pretty sure that this level of perfection is completely beyond my imagination."

"Good," he replied. "You deserve it after all those rounds of IVF."

"Do I sound like a total bitch?" she asked.

"Are you serious?"

"And I've totally come around to this place as well," she continued, turning and looking up at the imposing facade of their home. "I'm sorry I wasn't keen at the start, but I'm so glad you persuaded me to give it a try. Living out here in the middle of nowhere is such a great change from the city, and I'm sure Catherine's lungs are going to thank us in the long-term." She watched the windows of the house for a moment. "I know I joked about the place seeming creepy, but I don't think that anymore. It's such a bright, breezy and open home, I just feel like it's perfect." She smiled. "There's that word again. Perfect."

"This is the beginning of the rest of our lives," David told her, tousling the hair on top of her head before turning and heading inside. "And now, if you don't mind, I need to adjust the skirting boards in the dining room. Given the age of the house, it's not bad that the skirting board's the only thing I need to fix. *Then* the place will be perfect."

Smiling, Mia got to her feet and headed over to the pram. She reached down and adjusted the blanket, but Catherine was sleeping happily as if she had no cares in the world.

"My little miracle," Mia murmured, before looking out across the garden again and seeing the bucolic English countryside stretching to the horizon. "I've got a feeling we're going to be so happy here. Everything after this moment is going to be good for us as a family. Because after all the struggles, this moment – this exact moment – is absolutely perfect."

***

"So tell me honestly," David said a short while later, as Mia carried Catherine up the stairs and stopped on the landing, "look around and breathe it all in, and then I'm going to ask you a very important question."

"Okay," Mia replied, furrowing her brow, puzzled by her husband's request as she turned and looked all around.

"What do you see?" he asked.

"I see doors leading into the bedrooms," she replied.

"And?"

"I see... fresh wallpaper."

"And?"

"I see... light switches!"

"And?"

She turned to him.

"And?" he asked again.

"And what?"

"Do you see creepy shadows?"

She sighed.

"Do you see mysterious figures watching from a distance?"

"I never said that there were any -"

"Do you see ghosts?" he continued, stepping up behind her and putting his hands on the sides of her waist, before kissing the back of her neck gently. "Do you see anything at all that might even hint for one second that this house is in any way haunted?"

"No," she replied, "and I never actually said that it was."

"But you were worried," he pointed out, before taking a small notebook from his pocket and reaching around so that she could see the cover.

"That's why, over the past few months, I've been researching the history of every single person who ever lived in this house since it was built -"

"David..."

"Since it was built in the year 1884," he continued, finishing his sentence. "There are twenty-three names in this book, with twenty-three little biographies including twenty-three very mundane causes of death. No murders, no suicides, no horrific tragedies that might require vengeance. To be honest, I was actually a little disappointed." He kissed the side of her neck this time. "I think we might have moved into the most boring house in the whole of England."

"I'll take boring," she told him.

"I know that was one of your little concerns when we decided to move out here. You love your horror films and horror books, after all. So while no-one can conclusively prove that there are no ghosts, I can at least promise you that there *appears* to be nothing in this house's history that we should worry about." He set the notebook on a table near the top of the stairs. "I'm not belittling your fears, by the way," he added. "I'm taking them extremely seriously."

"Sure you are."

"No, I am!"

Catherine gurgled in her arms, as Mia turned to face her husband.

"I just want us to start properly here," David told her. "I want us to have a future in this house."

"I think things are looking very good in that department," she replied. "Like I said earlier, I'm getting amazing vibes from this place and any concerns I might have had are now long in the past. I've always been a city girl, I'm almost allergic to fresh smoke-free air, but I think I might just be able to handle the adjustment. I know I struggled a little bit during all the IVF treatment, but I'm over that now and I just want us to move on with our lives."

"So you're not worried that this place is haunted? Not even the teensiest bit?"

"Not for one second," she replied, placing a kiss on his cheek before looking down at the notebook. "Thank you for doing all that research, though. I'm looking forward to reading every word. For purely historical reasons, of course."

"Well, I think the house is pretty much sorted," he told her, "except for that gate out the front, which is going to need some serious work to stop it squeaking. I've tried all the usual stuff, but it just won't quit."

"I'm sure you'll figure it out," she replied as he made his way down the stairs. "Just don't obsess about it, okay?"

"Oh, I'm *definitely* going to obsess about it," he called back up to her as he hurried outside. "Do you know me at all? Obsessing about things is what I do!"

"There goes Daddy," Mia said with a smile, as she cradled Catherine in her arms and looked around. "Don't worry, he's not always quite this stressed about things. Not quite." She glanced down at the book and flipped it open, and she saw several names complete with relevant dates and short biographical notes. "He just wants to make sure that everything goes well now that we're a family, which makes you and I very lucky because it means we can focus on the most important things, like bonding and getting to know each other."

As if in response to that suggestion, Catherine let out a faint gurgle.

"That's right," Mia continued, looking down at her for a moment before kissing her on the forehead. "You've got nothing to worry about, my darling. Everything here is going to be perfect."

CHAPTER TWO

TWO WEEKS LATER, MIA stood at the kitchen sink and took a few seconds to scrub some particularly tough stains from the dinner plates.

"Honey?" David called out from the hallway. "I'm just going to check that gate again. It was creaking in the wind last night and I really don't want the same noise tonight."

"Okay," Mia said softly as she heard David's footsteps, followed by the sound of the front door opening and then bumping shut.

For the next few minutes she worked slowly but surely, cleaning the plates and cutlery before loading everything into the dishwasher. She always found something strangely calming about the rituals of dinnertime, from the preparation to the cooking and the eating, even through to tidying everything away; sometimes she worried that she was a little old-fashioned, but then she reminded herself that there perhaps wasn't anything wrong with being old-fashioned, and that old-fashioned ways had done previous generations just fine for hundreds of years.

Leaning down, she slid the last plate into the machine, and then – as she slipped a tablet into the drawer – she suddenly heard a loud thud coming from somewhere upstairs.

Standing up, she turned and looked over at the hallway.

"David?" she called out, even though she was fairly sure he hadn't come back inside. "Is that you?"

She waited, before heading over to the window and peering out to see that he was working on the gate at the end of the garden. She watched him opening and closing the gate several times, checking for the creaking sound, and then she flinched as she heard another bump coming from somewhere above. Looking up, she realized that the sound seemed to have come from somewhere up on the landing.

Furrowing her brow, she headed out into the hallway and walked into the front room, where she stopped to check that Catherine was still sleeping soundly.

"Hey there," she said, adjusting the blanket yet again, even though she knew it didn't really need adjusting at all. "Mummy's just being jumpy and -"

Before she could finish she heard a third bump, and this time as she looked back toward the hallway she felt a flicker of fear in her chest. No matter how hard she tried to tell herself that old houses habitually made strange noises, she couldn't shake the feeling that this particular trio of sounds – a heavy thud, then two bumps – sounded a little too much like there was someone up there. She checked on Catherine once more, before wandering out into the hallway and looking at the empty staircase.

She waited in silence, but now she heard nothing at all.

"Hello?" she called out cautiously. "Is someone there?"

She listened for a reply, and then she sighed as she realized that she was letting her imagination run wild. The house *was* old, and she had no doubt that there were a few gaps in the roof that would allow some gusts of wind to blow inside, and she figured that a few of these gusts must have caught a door or a window. Besides, she had no idea whether

David might have left a few windows open, so after a few seconds she turned to go back into the kitchen so she could finish the last of the clean-up job.

And then she stopped in the doorway as she heard a creaking sound coming from up on the landing, as if someone was carefully opening a door. Slowly, she turned and once again looked at the staircase.

***

Reaching the top of the stairs, Mia flicked the switch on the wall; the lights came on, and she looked around to see the doors to the three bedrooms as well as one more door that led into the bathroom. Two of the doors were open, while two had been left ajar, although she had no idea what they'd been like earlier.

"Hello?" she said again, even though she really hated the idea of giving voice to her fears. "Is anyone here?"

Once more the house stood in silence. Mia knew she should go downstairs, that searching the rooms would only heighten her sense of anxiety, but she still lingered for a moment. When she'd first laid eyes on the house she'd felt a shudder run through her bones, and her initial reaction had been that there was no way she could ever live in such an old, rundown place; then David had shown her the possibilities, and he'd promised to clean the place up before they moved in, and she'd gradually been able to banish any fear of the unknown.

Until now.

"Okay, then," she whispered, as she began to calm down a little. "I guess it was nothing."

Still she lingered, unable to ignore the sense that perhaps she'd missed something, that some element was wrong or out of place at the edge of her perception. She looked at each of the doors in turn, wondering what could be nagging at the back of her mind, and then she found herself staring at the blank wallpapered wall opposite. She blinked a couple of times, and then she made her way over and saw that some kind of dark smudge was now running vertically down the wall almost from the ceiling to the floor.

Reaching out, she was surprised to feel that the smudge was warm, and that some parts of the wallpaper had begun to blister slightly as if they'd been subjected to heat.

"What the hell?" she muttered, thinking back to earlier in the day, when she'd walked across the landing multiple times while doing the washing.

Although she couldn't be certain, she felt

fairly sure that earlier there had been no sign of any smudge. She touched the blisters again, and she was surprised to find that some of them were a little sticky; when she pulled her hand away, strands of liquefied paper remained attached to her fingertips.

"Okay, this *really* doesn't seem right," she murmured, before stepping back so that she could get a better view of the smudge, which if anything almost looked a little larger than before, and almost...

She tilted her head to one side.

Then to the other.

No.

No, she quickly told herself that she was wrong, that in fact the smudge in no way resembled the general shape of a person. She tilted her head again, trying to convince herself that she must be imagining things, yet in some way the smudge retained that general person-like hint. A moment later, hearing the front door swing open, she made her way to the top of the stairs and looked down just in time to see David heading back inside.

"That should do it," he said, setting a can of oil down on the table before removing his coat. "If not, I might have to take the whole thing off its hinges tomorrow and try something else."

"There's a burn mark on the wall up here,"

she told him.

"Huh?"

He looked up at her.

"On the wall between our bedroom and Catherine's nursery," she continued, turning to look at the smudge. "It's quite large, and I'm certain it wasn't there before. Some of the paper's even slightly bubbled. You don't think there could be something wrong with the wiring, do you?"

"I don't think there's anything behind that part of the wall."

"Well, there's definitely a mark."

"Do you smell anything odd?"

"No," she replied, watching the smudge for a moment longer before looking down at him again. "I suppose it's not too important, but we should probably get it looked at soon, just in case there's a problem. Do you think it could be caused by some weird kind of mold?"

"I wouldn't have thought so."

"Then what is it?"

"I'll take a look when I come up in a minute," he replied, making his way through to the downstairs bathroom. "Right now I really need to pee, and then I'm going to just sit in the front room and take the weight off my feet. Would you care to join me?"

"Sure," Mia replied as she heard the bathroom door swing shut.

Turning, she looked at the smudge again. Although she kept telling herself that there was no reason to worry, she couldn't deny that something about the mark on the wall made her feel uneasy; she hated not knowing what was happening in her own home, and the smudge seemed if anything to be standing out more than ever now, its darkness contrasting against the white of the rest of the wall. Every other part of the landing – of the entire house – had been freshly papered; now, for some reason, there was just one section on the landing that wasn't completely and utterly perfect.

CHAPTER THREE

HUNDREDS AND HUNDREDS OF nearly identical oats fell from the jar and cascaded down into the bowl.

"Are you coming to bed?" David asked from the doorway.

"Just a moment," Mia replied as she finished pouring out the oats, and then she set the jar down. "I just want to put these on to soak."

"I've been thinking about tomorrow," he continued. "If you're too tired for us to have Nick and Jackie over, I can totally put them off. I'll just come up with an excuse and they can go and get drunk somewhere else."

"Don't be silly," she replied, "I've been looking forward to it for ages. You know how much

I enjoy their company."

"Sure, but if it's too much stress or if you're finding it -"

"You're fussing too much," she added, interrupting him. "I've been looking forward to welcoming our first guests here for weeks. I've already bought all the food and planned everything out. I've got dinner all sorted, and drinks, and I've even got some ideas for entertainment. Honestly, after all the effort I've put in, I'd be really bummed if the night got canceled. In fact, I might even be a tad annoyed."

"You're not just putting on a brave face?"

She rolled her eyes.

"Well, I'm heading up," he said, sounding exhausted as he turned and wandered toward the stairs. "I'll settle Catherine down, but I know she's going to want a kiss from mummy before she'll settle."

"Yeah, I'll be right there," Mia said, taking the bowl over to the other counter before stopping as she saw a speck of darkness. "I just want to get everything sorted out ready for the morning, that's all. Things are chaotic enough already. I want a little more order."

Reaching down, she sifted through the oats and quickly found one that was a little discolored around the edges. Slipping it out from the pile, she held it up and saw that the discolored section was glistening; she touched that area and found to her puzzlement that it was a little soft, as if it had started to rot. At least the rest looked completely fine.

"Gross," she murmured, taking a moment to toss the offending oat into the bin before grabbing a bottle of milk and pouring some into the bowl, quickly submerging all the other oats. "Still, I guess there's always got to be one."

***

Flat on her back in bed, with the light off and the room shrouded in darkness, Mia stared up at the ceiling and wondered why she was still wide awake.

All evening she'd been exhausted, but as soon as she'd climbed into bed she'd suddenly felt wide awake and completely alert. That was par for the course in some ways, although it wasn't ideal with visitors arriving the next day; she knew the visit would be fun, but also that she'd end up absolutely exhausted by the end of the day, and their guests were staying overnight so things would be even more difficult. That was why, as she continued to stare up at the ceiling, she felt increasingly frustrated by her own inability to get some rest.

Hearing David let out a faint snort in his sleep, she turned to look over at him. She had to admit that she envied his ability to sleep, but she was determined to avoid taking any kind of drugs while she was breastfeeding, so sleeping pills were out. She wondered whether she could wake him up for sex, which was something that had always worked in the past, but for some reason the idea of sex filled her with a sense of loathing; she knew she was going to have to get over that, and that David was frustrated, yet in that moment she preferred to hold back. More than anything, she wanted to figure out how to flick the switch in her head that would bring her sex drive back.

Looking back up at the ceiling, she told herself that she was simply going to have to find some other way to tire her own mind. The last thing she needed was to spend hours and hours just going over her thoughts, so finally she began to sit up. David managed another snort, and in that moment Mia realized that she really only had one option.

***

As she reached the bottom of the stairs and finished tying the cord of her dressing gown, Mia already felt sleepy again, although this time she wasn't going to let herself get fooled. She knew that if she went straight back up to bed, she'd only end up in the same spot, so she forced herself to wander through to the kitchen and grab a glass of water.

Standing at the sink, she looked out at the darkness of the back garden, although in truth she could really only see her own reflection. She sipped some water while wondering what she could do to keep herself occupied at – she glanced over to the oven clock – one in the morning, and a moment later she realized that there was one very obvious solution. She knew she should get some milk out during the night anyway, so she wandered across the kitchen and grabbed the breast pump, and then she headed over to the dining room table.

At the last moment, realizing that she'd left both her phone and her book upstairs, she set the pump down and headed sleepily back to the hallway. Reaching the bottom of the stairs, she was about to go up when she suddenly heard the sound of a floorboard creaking in the kitchen.

She froze, looking past the stairs and watching the doorway. She could see one end of the kitchen table, and now her mind was racing as she tried to work out exactly what could have caused the floorboard to make such a loud and distinctive noise.

For a moment she considered calling out, but she quickly reminded herself of all her promises to David. She'd sworn that she wasn't going to start getting jumpy and paranoid in the new (old) house, so she forced herself instead to climb the stairs and go back to the bedroom. After checking on Catherine, she crept around to the table next to her own side and collected her book, and then she crept back to the door.

Behind her David let out another grunt, but Mia knew this was pretty normal for him.

Heading downstairs, she once again felt tired. Telling herself that she had to stay up until she was on the verge of passing out, she walked back through to the kitchen and sat at the table, and then she reached for the breast pump, only to find that it had vanished.

She looked around, and a moment later she spotted the pump standing on the counter near the sink.

Convinced that the pump had been on the table, she got to her feet and looked around the kitchen. All her earlier certainties were draining away now, and she couldn't help but worry that someone must have moved the pump. She slipped around the table and headed to the back door, double-checking that it was locked, and then she walked over to the counter and picked the pump up so she could check it wasn't damaged.

So far, so good.

Glancing around the kitchen again, she began to feel like a complete fool. Again. A twenty pound breast pump bought online didn't exactly feel like a traditional element in a horror story, yet she couldn't shake the worry that it couldn't have simply floated over to the counter. At the same time, she knew she was exhausted, and after a moment she realized that most likely she'd simply forgotten exactly what she'd been doing. That idea didn't feel quite right, but she supposed it was more likely than having some supernatural pump thief on the loose. Besides, her mind had been a little muddled ever since she'd given birth.

"Okay," she said, carrying the pump back to the table, "but if my nipple cream starts moving around, we're going to have words."

After taking a seat, she took a few minutes to set the pump up and then she began to express milk, squeezing the plunger while telling herself that she'd be glad of the extra milk in the morning. She felt slightly foolish, but the pump produced various noises that at least helped to puncture any sense of foreboding. In fact, as she continued to express, she began to lose all sense of fear, and instead she realized that she was starting to feel pretty tired. She looked around the kitchen, wondering how she could possibly have let herself become spooked, and then she focused on simply getting out as much milk as possible.

And then, hearing a scratching sound, she glanced across the room and looked at one of the cabinets. In that instant, she saw the reflection of a woman standing out in the hallway.

"What the -"

Pulling the breast pump aside, she got to her feet just as the woman stepped out of view. Hurrying across the kitchen, Mia looked out into the hallway, but there was absolutely no sign of anyone at all; she made her way to the stairs and hurried up, rushing into the bedroom and heading straight to the cot, where she found to her relief that Catherine was still fast asleep. Picking up her daughter, she cradled her in her arms as she hurried to the bed and nudged her husband.

"David!" she hissed as he began to groggily wake from deep sleep. "There's an intruder! David, I'm not kidding! There's a woman downstairs in our house!"

CHAPTER FOUR

"THERE'S NO WOMAN DOWNSTAIRS in our house," David said, stopping at the foot of the staircase and looking up at Mia, who was sitting halfway up with Catherine still in her arms. "Seriously. I've checked everywhere at least twice."

"I'm not crazy," she replied, glaring back down at him as she held Catherine tighter than ever. "David! I'm not!"

"I never said you were crazy," he responded, before pausing as he realized that he had to pick his words with care. "I think perhaps you're tired and -"

"I'm not tired!" she snapped. "I mean, I *am*, but that's not what happened here. I saw a woman, David, and she was watching me while I... while I was pumping milk!"

"That seems a little odd," he pointed out.

"I'm not disagreeing with you on that!" she hissed.

"Let's just calm down," he said, holding up his hands as Catherine gurgled. "Mia, I've checked every single room multiple times, and I've done it in a way that means nobody could have doubled back on me and hidden. I've checked the doors and windows, and the attic as well, plus we don't even have a basement so there's no need to worry about that."

"How do you know we don't have a basement?" she asked.

"We just don't!"

"Isn't that odd?"

"It's not the oddest thing in the world," he replied. "Not *every* house has a basement. Some of them just have a big old set of foundations. Mia, I think we're focusing on the wrong thing here. You got up in the night to express some milk, which is great, but you're sleep-deprived so you very briefly imagined a shape that your brain interpreted as a figure."

She started shaking her head.

"And then we got to this point," he added, "and I completely understand your concern, but I think we need to slow down and just focus on the facts."

Catherine's gurgles began to turn into the start of cries.

"Catherine's getting upset," he pointed out. "All three of us are knackered and -"

"I know what I saw, David," Mia said firmly. "It wasn't some kind of illusion, it was an actual person. I might not have made out her face, but I could tell from the silhouette that it was a woman."

"Then it was probably a reflection."

"Not *my* reflection!" she protested angrily, before Catherine started to cry properly. "Hey there," she cooed, rocking the girl gently, "there's no need to get upset. Mummy's sorry she raised her voice, but you really have nothing to worry about. You're completely safe." She glanced at David. "I won't let anyone get near her," she continued. "Whoever that woman was, even if you don't believe me, I'm not going to leave Catherine alone even for a second."

"You barely do anyway," he murmured under his breath.

"What did you just say?"

"Nothing," he continued, returning his voice to full volume. "Listen, why don't you settle Catherine back down. I can put away the pump and all that stuff in the kitchen." He waited for her to respond. "Please, Mia?" he added plaintively. "I'm just done for tonight, okay? I'm knackered and I need some sleep. Listen, are you sure you don't want me to call off the visit tomorrow? If you're not feeling it, we can reschedule to another weekend. You know they won't mind, they'll just go off partying in Brighton like they do every other weekend. You don't have to feel bad, I can just tell them that this weekend isn't convenient."

"And how would you explain that?" she asked, clearly bristling at the suggestion. "Would you tell them that I've lost the plot and you don't think we can handle visitors? Is that what you'd do? Would you just throw me under the bus?"

"Of course not."

"Don't cancel," she said firmly. "I mean it. If you cancel, I'll just feel like even more of an idiot."

"You're not an idiot," he told her. "You never could be. You're just stressed by parenthood. We both are."

"I can't believe you don't believe me," she replied, getting to her feet and starting to carry Catherine upstairs. "I never realized that you thought I was some kind of lunatic."

"I don't!" he protested. "I'm just trying to be the logical one here!" He waited for a reply, but as his wife made her way into the bedroom he realized that he might have said the wrong thing again. "I didn't phrase that quite right," he continued. "Mia? I didn't mean to imply that you're *not* logical, I'm just playing devil's advocate for a moment. There's really, very clearly nobody else down here."

Sighing, he realized that there was no point

trying to reason with her.

"There just isn't," he added, even though he knew nobody else could hear him now. He looked around and saw the doors to the living room, the dining room and the kitchen, as well as the front door. "There just... isn't!"

***

"Baby's favorite," David said a few minutes later as he put the last of the bottles in the fridge. "You're a lucky kid, Catherine. You've got a great mother, and if I might say so, a not so terrible father as well."

He was about to shut the fridge door, but at the last moment he hesitated. Glancing across the room, he saw the pump on the table, but there was no sign of Mia and he felt sure his wife was upstairs still tucking Catherine back in for the night; he turned to the bottles again, and he could already feel a growing sense of curiosity niggling at the back of his mind. Finally, reaching out, he took one of the bottles and pulled the lid away.

After hesitating for a few seconds, he took a tiny sip of the milk, before swirling it around his mouth for a few seconds and then swallowing.

"Huh," he murmured, clearly a little surprised by the taste. "Kinda... sweet."

He took another sip, before setting the lid back in place and putting the bottle on the shelf, then swinging the fridge door shut.

"And... let's never tell anyone I did that," he muttered, before heading to the table and reaching for the pump.

Stopping suddenly, he saw that there was no sign of the pump at all. He looked around, but to his surprise it seemed to have completely vanished, even though he knew for certain that it had been right there on the table just a few seconds earlier.

"Mia?" he said cautiously. "Honey, are you down here?"

He waited.

Silence.

"If you just saw me do that," he continued, "I was only... curious. I know it's a little on the weird side, and I'm sorry, but I'm pretty sure every guy has a taste at least once. And it wasn't bad at all. I almost liked it."

Again he waited, but now he was starting to realize that there was no sign of her. A moment later he heard her walking from one room to another upstairs, and then as he glanced across the kitchen he saw that the breast pump was on the counter near the sink.

"Huh," he said, furrowing his brow. "How did you get over..."

Making the way to the sink, he picked the pump up and turned it around in his hands, trying to work out how it could possibly have transported itself all the way across the room. He turned and looked over at the table, but the distance was far too great for there to be any reasonable explanation, so he realized finally that he simply must have been mistaken.

"Mia's not the only one who's losing it tonight," he said, taking a moment to clean the pump before setting it on the side to dry.

Sighing, he switched the kitchen light off and headed to the door, before stopping at the last moment. As if he'd perhaps picked up on something at the edge of his senses, he slowly turned and looked back across the room, keeping the light off as he watched the shadows. He wasn't even sure what he was waiting for, yet he lingered for a few more seconds before his gaze fell upon the back door. Finally he headed over and checked one last time that the door was properly locked, before walking back to the doorway. He stopped again, and again he looked over his shoulder, but this time – satisfied that there was no-one around – he switched off the hall light and began to make his way up the stairs.

For the next few minutes, the kitchen remained dark and still, with no sign of movement at all. The fridge hummed slightly, but otherwise the room was silent. Finally, a shadowy figure stepped out from the pantry and stood watching the scene.

CHAPTER FIVE

"THAT'S TOTALLY NOT WHAT happened," Jackie said the following evening, holding a glass of wine as she leaned back in her chair at the dinner table. "David fell out of the tree *after* everyone had seen him through the window."

"Okay," David said with a smile, "I think I should clarify a few details of this story before I end up sounding like a complete tool."

"We're way past that moment," Nick interjected.

"This is my favorite story from our college days," Jackie continued. "Mia, honestly, if you'd known David back then you'd have seen a very different side to him."

"I can't believe there was a time when he struggled to talk to girls," Mia replied. "The David I met a few years ago was so suave and sophisticated. I mean, when we first got talking in that bar and he told me all about how he'd switched from science to art in his career, I was swept up in the whole thing. I thought he was this amazing guy who could probably pick up any girl he wanted in the whole world. Honestly, I just couldn't believe that he was interested in me at all."

"So he was hiding in a tree perving on this girl," Jackie replied, "and -"

"That is totally not what was happening," David protested, struggling not to laugh. "I'd actually climbed up there because I wanted to take a photo of a nearby cemetery, and I had no idea that those girls from our English class lived in the house next door." He moved his wine glass to his lips, ready to take a sip, before hesitating. "Or that Sabrina Oakenshaw was going to be changing by the window at that exact moment. Or that she'd be... taking off her top, and applying fake tan to her chest. Or that she'd choose that moment to look out the window, just as I happened to glance in her direction while holding my camera."

"It was like something from *Back to the Future*," Nick chuckled.

"I straightened it all out with them," David explained.

"And with the police."

"They called the police?" Mia said, her eyes

opening wide with amused shock. "How did I never hear this part of the story? What kind of -"

Before she could finish, they all heard a very loud thud coming from the room above, as if something heavy had hit the ground. As they looked up, Catherine began to cry upstairs.

"I'll go," Mia said quickly, setting her napkin aside and getting to her feet.

"I'm sure it's nothing," David replied, reaching out to put a hand on her wrist. "Don't -"

In that instant he knocked his own wine glass, sending red wine splashing off the side of the table and splattering his wife's dress.

"Thanks," Mia said, clearly not impressed.

"I'm sorry," he sighed, getting to his feet as the last of the wind splattered down onto the floor. "Damn it, I never used to be clumsy before."

"That'll be parenthood for you," Jackie said with a grin. "You see? This is one of the many reasons I've never wanted kids!"

"I'm so sorry," Mia told her, before turning to David as Catherine continued to cry upstairs. "You clean this up, and I'll go and check on Catherine. I'm sure you're right, I'm sure it's nothing, but I have to make sure."

"Bring her down!" Jackie called after her as she hurried out of the room. "Let her see how her favorite godparents eat at a fancy dinner party!"

"Maybe," Mia said, making her way up the

stairs as she examined her dress and saw a large wine stain. "Hang on, I'll need to change too. I'll be back down in just a jiffy!"

***

"So how are things going these days?" Jackie said somewhat pointedly, as she watched David wiping up the spilled wine. "Is it too soon to ask?"

"Everything's fine," he replied, dabbing at the puddle next to the chair leg. "It's all in the past."

"Are you sure about that?" she continued. "Don't me wrong, I'm glad if that's true, but I wasn't aware that people could get over stuff like that so quickly."

"Maybe this isn't the right moment to bring it up," Nick said, nudging her arm. "Come on... Seriously?"

"It's fine," David said, wiping some more of the wine away. "We've always been very open about what happened. Yes, Mia struggled a *lot* with the IVF treatment and there were some associated mental health issues that needed to be addressed. Which she did, by the way. I'm very proud of how she handled herself, and of the way she confronted the problems she was having. Yes, things got bad for a while, but they could have been so much worse. And now everything's fine."

"And how many cycles of IVF did she end

up having, again?"

"Jackie..."

"Ten?"

He sighed.

"Fifteen?"

He sighed again.

"Twenty?" she added, clearly shocked. "David, where did the money come from? Why would any doctor agree to so many procedures? Are you seriously telling me that she went through twenty cycles?"

"I'm not saying that at all," he told her. "I'm not commenting. It was... more than three, but less than twenty. Let's just leave it at that. And I paid for it because my investments have been doing really well lately, and because my last art show was a big success."

"I still can't believe you're an artist," Nick said, clearly trying to change the subject before Jackie could ask any more personal questions about the IVF. "Hey, do you ever think about what your life would have been like if you'd stuck it out on your original course? I heard you were a star pupil, you could be one of the top quantum physicists in the world by now."

"I hated every second of that course," he pointed out, getting to his feet. "I only did it because my dad pressured me."

"And then you dropped out after less than a

year," Jackie reminded him, "and incurred the great man's wrath forever by switching to study painting and art and all that stuff he considered to be completely unimportant. When was the last time you talked to him, anyway? How does he feel now that you can sell your paintings at twenty grand a pop?"

"It's been a while," he replied awkwardly, as he refilled his wine glass from the bottle on the table. He paused, and now a faint smile reached his lips. "And yes, he's still furious about my career in art. I swear, no matter how well I do, he'll always be thinking about how I could have done better if I'd stuck to physics."

"Yeah, but you'd be miserable," Nick said. "Art's in your blood. Plus, you actually make good money from it, and we all know how rare and difficult that is."

"I never much fancied the starving artist trope," David admitted.

"Just think, though," Jackie replied. "If you were some high-flying physicist, you could have afforded a hundred IVF cycles!"

"Will you leave him alone?" Nick hissed.

"We didn't need a hundred," David said, holding his glass up for a toast, "because after the number we tried, even though the doctors told us we had no chance, we got our own little miracle. I have to admit, I would have given up if Catherine hadn't insisted on trying again and again, and even with all the time and all the money we still needed a stroke of the most unimaginable luck." He held his glass out a little further. "To miracles."

"To miracles," Jackie and Nick both said as they leaned forward and clinked their glasses.

Looking up at the ceiling, David realized that Catherine had stopped crying.

"And that's *another* miracle," he continued. "She's such a great baby, she rarely cries and when she does, Mia's always able to calm her down really quickly."

"So the depression didn't come back?" Jackie asked, before Nick nudged her arm again. "What?" she protested. "I just want to be sure that Mia's not slipping back into her old pre-baby habits, and it's not like I asked in front of her! Postpartum depression's a real thing, guys, and it can have horribly serious consequences! My concern is absolutely coming from a place of love!"

"Which I appreciate," David told her, "but the honest truth is that no, she hasn't had any setbacks at all. In fact, she's really been flourishing since Catherine was born. I know how corny and maybe even backward this might sound, and I'm not saying it's true of all or even most women, but for Mia... I really, truly believe from the bottom of my heart that Mia was born to be a mother. You might almost say that it's her calling in life."

CHAPTER SIX

"THERE YOU GO," MIA said, settling Catherine back down in her crib as the girl let out a brief laugh. "Mummy's little sweetheart doesn't need to be scared. I don't know what that loud bump was, but I promise you it was nothing horrible."

She tickled up Catherine's chin, causing the child to laugh again.

"You know I love you, right?" she continued. "More than any mummy has ever loved any baby. You're my whole world, Catherine, and there's nothing I wouldn't do for you. I'd even -"

Catching herself just in time, she realized she was in danger of sounding just a little morbid.

"Well, I don't need to say it out loud," she added with a grin. "The point is, you don't ever have to worry about anything, because Mummy will always be right here for you."

She tickled her chin again, and again Catherine giggled.

"You really love that, don't you?" Mia said. "Listen, I'd better change and get back downstairs for this boring dinner party, but I think you're better off here. The baby monitor's all set up, so if you need anything, just gurgle and I'll come running. Honestly, I would run across burning coals for you. I know that sounds a little dramatic, but as far as I'm concerned it's not even dramatic *enough*." She paused, staring down at her daughter for a moment longer. "I would let the rest of the world burn just to save you. I'd give up everything I have, even my own life, just to make sure that you're alright. There's really no limit to what I'd do for you, Catherine."

She brushed the edge of a finger against the girl's cheek, causing her to let out another gurgled laugh. For a few seconds Mia felt absolutely transfixed, as if she could never break her gaze away from her daughter; sometimes she felt annoyed by anyone or anything else that demanded her attention, even for a moment, and she wondered why she couldn't spend every hour of every day just focused entirely on being a mother. Even though she knew that aim was unrealistic, part of her still resented any distraction that ever rolled along.

"I should get changed," she added, finally

pulling back and heading into the dressing room. "Mummy's just through here," she added as she slipped the dress over her head and set it down, before walking to the wardrobe and starting to find another. "Don't worry, I'll be sure to get your opinion on whatever dress I choose."

She began to look at the various dresses on different hangers, but at first nothing really jumped out at her.

"Of course, Daddy just *had* to spill on my favorite dress, didn't he?" She checked a couple more, before pulling one out and holding it for a quick inspection. "I suppose this one'll be fine," she said, turning it around and then starting to slip it over her head.

She took a moment to pull the dress down, but then – as she was about to check that it was all fine – she froze as she heard Catherine giggling again. When the giggling turned to laughter, she couldn't help furrowing her brow, since she knew that Catherine only ever reacted that way when she had company.

"Honey?"

Heading over to the doorway, she stopped and looked over at the crib. She could see Catherine wriggling at the bottom, but a moment later a shadow moved across the far wall and shifted out of view.

"What the hell?"

Rushing forward, Catherine raced over to the crib just in time to see the shadow disappearing across the landing. Hurrying to the doorway, she looked out past the stairs, but now there was no sign of anyone. She opened her mouth to call out, but at that moment she heard laughter coming from downstairs and she realized that everyone was still at the dinner table. She looked across the landing again, but she already knew that she'd end up looking like a complete fool if she started telling the others about moving shadows.

Stepping back over to the bedroom, she looked at the crib again, and then she saw the baby monitor on the nearby table. If anyone else had been in the room, the monitor would have picked it up and David would have heard downstairs, so after a few seconds she was able to convince herself that there was really no need to worry.

"You're not crazy," she whispered, figuring that she simply needed to get her dress sorted out and go back downstairs. "You've got this. Your life is perfect and you're not going to pull it apart just because of an over-active imagination. No way."

***

"Who's a cute baby?" Jackie cooed as she held Catherine up a short while later, down in the kitchen. She swung her around, causing the girl to let out another brief laugh. "Who's the cutest baby in the whole world?"

"She likes you," Mia said with a smile as she rinsed another plate and loaded it into the dishwasher. "I can tell."

"She'd *better* like me," Jackie continued, swinging Catherine around some more. "In fact, I'd better be her favorite non-parent person in the whole world. Does she even know about that buggy I bought for you guys when she was born?"

"I told you that was too much," Mia replied. "You've already been way too generous."

"It was nothing."

"I looked up online how much those buggies cost," Mia told her. "I know I shouldn't have, but you really went way too far."

"Oh, just let me live vicariously through you guys," Jackie said, dancing with Catherine across the kitchen, still holding her up in the air. "I might never want kids of my own, but that doesn't mean I don't like to play with them, tire them out and then hand them back to their poor over-worked parents. Really, I think that's win-win for everyone."

"Just don't get her too excited right before bedtime."

"You see?" Jackie said, looking up at Catherine with a grin as she held her higher and higher. "That's the difference between mummies and godparents. Mummies worry about everything and try to put the kibosh on all the fun, whereas godparents swing you around and let you go a little bit crazy." She spun her clockwise for a moment, then anti-clockwise. "Now tell me, young Catherine, which you prefer."

In response, Catherine began to laugh as if being flung around in the air was the funniest thing that had ever happened to her.

"I know which I'd prefer," Jackie laughed. "I'm not even sure it'd be that hard to -"

Suddenly she half-tripped on a bag that had been left on the floor. Stumbling forward, she just about managed to stay on her feet, but in the process she fell forward and slammed Catherine straight into one of the cupboards.

"Shit!" Jackie gasped, turning Catherine around as the baby began to scream. "I'm so sorry!"

"Let me take a look," Mia said, rushing over and gathering Catherine into her arms. "Hey, let Mummy see what happened. Don't worry, everything's going to be alright."

"I don't think she actually hit anything," Jackie said. "I'm sorry, Mia! Hey, at least there's no blood!"

"Don't be, she's fine," Mia replied, as she continued to check Catherine over. "I think you're right, she didn't actually hit the cupboard, she's probably just shocked." She held her daughter close and stroked her on the back. "It's okay, Catherine," she continued, "there's no need to be scared. Aunt Jackie just stumbled, that's all."

"I'm not drunk," Jackie replied. "I mean, I *am* drunk, but that's not why I tripped. You know I can handle my wine, right?"

"I know," Mia said, kissing the side of Catherine's head as the girl continued to cry at the top of her lungs. "Honestly, it's all fine, she just got a little bit of a fright but it's nothing she won't get over." She patted Catherine's back again as she began to carry her to the door. "However, I think this might be her cue to retire for the night. She's already had way too much excitement for one night."

"Totally," Jackie said. "I know that when *I* start bawling my eyes out, that's usually when I should make my excuses and leave the party." She held up a hand and waved. "Goodnight, Catherine," she continued, "sorry about almost giving you a concussion. Hey, in the morning let's have some more conventional playtime, and I'll remind you again why I'm still the best godparent any kid ever had in their life."

She waited as Mia carried Catherine out into the hallway, and then she leaned back against the counter and let out a big, long sigh.

"Well done, Jackie," she said, rolling her eyes, "you damn near brained the kid. Just another example of why it's a good job you're not responsible for anything more demanding than a goldfish."

CHAPTER SEVEN

"YOUR LIFE'S REALLY PERFECT, isn't it?" Nick said as he sat in the conservatory at the rear of the house, sipping from his fourth glass of wine. "Sorry, I don't mean to sound jealous, it's just... you've got it all worked out."

"I wouldn't say that, exactly," David replied, looking out the window and watching the lawn for a moment. "I don't think anyone's life is ever *perfect*, everyone has little problems and stress factors, although I have to admit that we perhaps have fewer that most people."

"Okay," Nick continued, "but if it's not perfect for you, it's definitely perfect for Mia. You go out of your way to make sure that she doesn't have to worry about anything. I've honestly never seen any woman ever look so happy."

"You're right about that," David said, tipping the last of the wine into his glass before getting to his feet. "I'd do anything for her, though. All I care about is walking through that front door every day and seeing a happy, smiling Mia. Hang on, I'll grab another bottle."

"You alright there?" Nick asked as he watched him leaving the room. "You're looking a little unsteady on your feet."

"I'm not used to drinking these days," David explained, holding onto the jamb for support as he stepped through into the kitchen. "Damn it, I used to be able to knock back ten times more than this when we were at college. When did we all start getting old?"

"Tell me about it," Nick muttered, looking out the window as he took another sip. "I don't even have kids and I feel like I'm about ninety."

He was about to turn away, when at the last moment he spotted a figure out at the far end of the garden. Squinting, he watched as a woman wearing a ragged dress shuffled along the path leading toward the house. At first he wondered whether he was simply imagining things, but as the woman edged closer and closer he began to sit up and take a little more notice. He blinked a couple of times, half expecting the woman to turn out to be some kind of alcohol-induced mirage.

"Hey, David," he called out, "do you have

somebody else staying here?"

"What was that?" David replied from far off in the kitchen.

"Do you have like... an old woman staying here?" Nick continued, getting to his feet and peering outside, only to find that there was no longer any sign of the stranger at all. "Or maybe living in your garden like some kind of weird shaman? Huh, that's weird. She's gone now."

"Who's gone?"

Nick turned to him, clearly on the verge of adding to his claim, before at the last second he sighed and shook his head.

"Forget it," he continued. "You know what? I'm a complete idiot and I think I just hallucinated something straight out of a horror story. How strong's this wine, anyway? You didn't break and give me the good stuff, did you?"

"Not you too," David muttered, rolling his eyes as he wandered over with a freshly-opened bottle of wine. "I had enough of that sort of thing with..." He paused as he set the bottle down. "Sorry, I shouldn't talk about that," he added. "I promised Mia I wouldn't go on about all the IVF stuff and the problems she had when she was pregnant, and I should be a dutiful husband and respect that promise. All I ever wanted in life was a happy wife and a happy child, and I've got that." He began to top up their glasses. "I should learn to be more like

Mia. She's content with what she's got. There's no need to always be trying to make things better. If you chase perfection all the time, you'll never stop to enjoy what you've already got."

"Amen to that," Nick replied, waiting until his glass was full again before taking a sip. "And by the way, might I compliment you on your excellent taste in wine? I've gotta hand it to you, David. You really know your bottles."

"It's not an easy thing to master," David admitted, as he finished topping up his own glass. "There can be big differences based on the vintages, even if everything else seems the same."

"Cheers to being content with our lot in life," Nick said, holding his glass up. "Here's to the good times."

***

"Hmm, what?"

Rolling over in the bed in the guest room, Jackie opened her eyes. She felt sure that her husband Nick had just said something, but as she looked at him in the darkness she realized that he was actually sound asleep. She waited, furrowing her brow, yet now she was starting to think that perhaps she'd experienced some kind of waking dream.

"And now I need to pee," she muttered,

annoyed by her own bladder as she climbed out of bed. "I swear I'm turning more and more into my own mother."

She made her way around the bed and over to the door. After listening for a moment to make sure that no-one else was up and about, she pulled the door open and slipped out onto the landing; she gently bumped the door shut again before heading over toward the bathroom, but at the last moment she stopped at the top of the stairs as she spotted movement out of the corner of her eye.

Looking down at the darkened hallway, she told herself that she must have been wrong, yet the impression of someone walking through into the dining room had been very distinct.

She waited, half-expecting a light to turn on downstairs, but as the seconds passed she couldn't shake the fear that something might actually be wrong. She knew that Nick was asleep, and although she figured that perhaps Mia was up and about doing something motherly, she couldn't quite ignore a niggling concern in the back of her mind. Finally, figuring that she simply had to ignore her concerns, she turned and headed to the bathroom.

Three minutes later, as she headed back to the guest room, she stopped at the top of the stairs again. This time she'd heard a bump, as if somebody had knocked a chair; in fact, she recognized the sound as the exact same noise she'd heard at dinner whenever anyone had moved a chair, with the legs scraping against the lino in the kitchen. She knew that she should be able to see a hint of light if anyone had made their way down there, and after a moment she began to wonder who could possibly be sneaking around downstairs in the darkness.

She hesitated, but this time she couldn't help herself; she began to make her way down, while bracing herself for David or Mia or perhaps even Nick to suddenly step into view and give her the fright of her life.

"Let's not have any jump-scares, thank you very much," she said under her breath.

Once she was in the hallway, she stopped and looked around. The house seemed completely still, yet she felt a tingling sensation on the back of her neck as if she could somehow tell she was being observed. She turned and looked at each of the doors in turn, before stopping as her gaze fell upon the open doorway leading into the kitchen. Stepping forward, she looked through and saw moonlight streaming through the far window, picking out the table where – just a few hours earlier – they'd all sat for their loud and slightly boozy meal. There was no sign of anyone now, of course, yet this still wasn't quite enough to allay her concerns.

Stepping a little further into the kitchen, she looked around, and finally she spotted a figure standing in the shadows at the far end of the room.

"Mia?" she gasped, letting out a sigh of relief. "You scared me half to death. Sorry, I didn't mean to come creeping around down here. You're gonna laugh, but I just got a little spooked, that's all."

Making her way to the sink, she poured herself a glass of water.

"Might as well hydrate while I'm down here," she added with a smile, before downing the glass and then giving it a quick rinse. "Nick's always going on about how I have to stay hydrated. Do you remember when hydrating was just called drinking water? Sometimes I long for the simpler times."

Once she'd finished washing the glass, she set it down and turned to see that Mia hadn't moved at all. In fact, the more she stared across the darkened kitchen, the more Jackie began to wonder if the woman *was* Mia. She certainly couldn't see the other person's face, since her hair was pulled almost entirely over her features; in some ways she seemed to be Mia but in other ways she didn't, and Jackie felt a sense of concern starting to slowly rise up through her chest.

"Are you okay, Mia?" she asked cautiously, before spotting the breast pump on the table. "Oh, I'm so sorry, did I interrupt you? Do you have to get up and do that in the night as well? Sorry, I didn't know. I don't really have the motherly knowledge down."

She began to make her way to the door, before slowing her pace and stopping again. Turning and staring at the figure, she realized that there had been no response since she'd entered the kitchen, and she still couldn't be quite certain that this was Mia at all. She hesitated, before stepping over to the light switch and reaching out.

"I'm just going to pop this on for a moment," she said, looking at the switch as she gave it a flick, filling the kitchen with light. She stared at the switch for a few more seconds, before realizing that the figure had stepped right up up behind her. "Is that okay, Mia?" she asked nervously. "Do you mind?"

Turning, she saw that the woman was just a few inches away. Hair was still covering the person's face, although one eye was glaring out at her through a gap.

"Mia, *is* that you?" Jackie said cautiously, before reaching out and parting the hair so she could see the woman's face. She stared for a moment, before letting out a sigh of relief. "Oh! Damn! Okay, it's -"

CHAPTER EIGHT

"THE OFFICE?" NICK SAID the following morning, standing in the kitchen and reading the note again. "I don't get it, why would she have to rush back to the office at the crack of dawn? And why didn't she take her phone?"

"I thought Jackie was glued to that thing," David said, carrying a few more items over to the breakfast table. "I don't think I've ever seen her without it since mobiles became a thing. Hey, are you going to try my homemade marmalade?"

"She must have forgotten it," Nick suggested, looking over at the phone. "That's so unlike her, but I suppose it happens to everyone occasionally. Whatever the office wanted, it must have been really important for her to shoot off like this. I didn't even hear the car leaving. Then again, I always sleep with earplugs in these days. I don't really have a choice, Jackie could snore for England."

"Has anyone seen my pump?" Mia muttered, still searching through one of the cupboards. "I swear it was here last night, I always put it in the exact same place."

"Sorry," David replied, setting some croissants on a baking tray. "Jackie's loss, I guess. More breakfast for the rest of us. You're going to love my homemade marmalade. I'm actually wondering whether I've found a new calling in life. I've got a real knack for making the stuff. I do it in these batches, it drives Mia crazy but I find it strangely meditative."

"It's always here," Mia continued, sounding increasingly annoyed as she checked the others shelves in the cupboard. "I specifically remember putting it in its usual place last night, and I didn't come down to express in the night because I didn't think I needed to, and now it's gone."

"Do you need to express right now?" David asked.

"No, but -"

"Then there'll be time to find it after breakfast," he continued, interrupting her before she could finish. He took a moment to slide the tray into the oven before turning to her. "Listen, it's going to be around here somewhere. It has to be. So if you don't need it right now, what's the problem?"

"That's not the point," she replied, and now she seemed extremely flustered. "There's no way Jackie could have taken it with her, is there?"

"Why would Jackie take a breast pump?" David said.

They both turned to Nick.

"I really don't think Jackie's into baby paraphernalia," he told them. "Seriously, guys, I've seen that pump. It's not like you could mistake if for anything else."

"Then where is it?" Mia asked, putting a hand on the side of her face and tucking some hair behind her ear. "I don't want to have to order another one, it's so wasteful. And it'd take a few days to come, so I'd probably just have to go into town and buy one there anyway."

"Or you could just..."

David's voice trailed off for a moment as she turned to him.

"Do it the normal way?" he suggested cautiously, clearly worried that he might be about to say something wrong. "The way God intended?"

"Of course I can do that," she told him with a heavy sigh. "It's just the principle, and it's the fact that I hate things vanishing like this."

"Stuff goes missing," David told her. "That's just part of life. This morning I went to the shed and I got a few things so I can adjust a shelf in the front room, and I noticed that a few of my power tools were totally not where I left them. And one of the little old hacksaws was gone. Do you see me stressing over it, though? No, you don't. Because I simply accept that the hacksaw will turn up sooner rather than later. Besides, it was rusty as hell, so I won't even miss it that much. I view this as the universe's way of telling me to get some new tools."

As Mia took a deep breath, she heard Catherine giggling over the baby monitor.

"I have to find that pump," Mia said after a moment. "I know it might sound silly to you guys, but I just can't stand not knowing where it is or why it's been moved. I always keep things so organized, I have to or everything just goes wrong, and I can't handle having confusion." She checked the cupboard again before letting out a sigh of irritation. "I need things to be where I left them. I need everything to be absolutely perfect."

"I bet it'll show up after breakfast," David said, stepping over and placing a hand on her shoulder. "You just need to chill out."

"Don't patronize me," she replied, turning to him.

Over the baby monitor, Catherine giggled again.

"Sshh!" a voice gasped suddenly, also emerging from the monitor's speakers.

"Did you hear that?" Mia asked, before

turning and racing out of the room. "Somebody's up there with Catherine!"

***

"I checked every single room," David said a few minutes later, as he walked back through into the bedroom, "and there's no sign of anyone."

"And I checked downstairs," Nick added, following him from the landing. "Guys, there's no-one else here."

"You heard it!" Mia hissed, holding Catherine close in her arms as she turned to them. "You both heard that voice!"

"I heard... something," David admitted cautiously, "but it wasn't necessarily a distinct voice. It could have been anything."

"Exactly," Nick said. "Sure, it sounded like someone was shushing Catherine, but in reality there are probably a million things that could have caused that noise."

"Name one," Mia replied.

"A fly," he continued. "What if a fly landed on the monitor, and its little legs or something brushed the microphone, and that caused a kind of rustling sound that we interpreted as a human voice? I don't know what the microphone on a baby monitor's like, exactly, but it's probably small, and flies have these really scratchy legs that'd probably make weird sounds if they touched it in a certain way. I know it sounds crazy and unlikely, but what's the alternative?"

"The alternative," Mia said, "is -"

She caught herself just in time, before kissing the side of Catherine's head again.

"There's no such thing as ghosts," David said firmly. "We've talked about this before. Ghosts aren't real, and even if they were, there wouldn't be any in this house."

"I know," she replied.

"But it's what you're thinking," he continued. "Trust me, I can almost read your mind at this point. I think this is a really dangerous thought process to pursue, and I want us to stop before we advance any further along that path. Slightly mixed metaphors aside, Nick's right, there's bound to be a perfectly reasonable explanation for that sound we heard. Just because we don't know what that explanation is, and just because we might never figure it out, doesn't mean that it doesn't exist." He paused. "Tell her, Nick."

"Hmm?" Nick replied, looking up from his phone. "Sorry, I was just texting the guys from the office to see if they know why Jackie had to head off so early. I know I shouldn't worry, but it's so weird that she didn't take her phone. This thing has her emails, her calendar, her socials... it has everything on it. She's more likely to accidentally leave the house naked than forget her phone."

"Did you look at that little book I gave you?" David asked as he stepped over to Mia. "Do you remember the one I used to jot down details about all the people who ever lived in this house before us?"

"I really don't think that's going to help," she told him.

"And Catherine seems fine," he added, stroking the back of the baby's head. "Think about it for one moment, Mia. If some scary ghost had shown up, don't you think that Catherine would have been upset? Wouldn't she have cried? Instead she seems completely fine, in fact I don't see so much as a sliver of worry on her face. So come on, apply some logic here, if there was really a ghost then Catherine wouldn't be taking it so well. Would she?"

"No," Mia said cautiously, although she still seemed a little reluctant to admit that he had a point. "I know," she added with a sigh, "it's just -"

Before she could finish, they all heard the doorbell ringing downstairs.

"I'll get it," David said, turning and heading out of the room. "I've been waiting for a package, hopefully it's finally shown up. Last time the stupid delivery company decided our recycling bin was a safe spot to put it, and I never saw the damn thing again."

Mia leaned down and kissed the top of Catherine's head again, before glancing at the window and realizing she could see a hint of flashing blue lights outside. Making her way past David, who was still tapping at his phone, she looked out and saw to her surprise that a couple of police cars were parked a few hundred feet away, out by the side of the road that ran past the house. She watched as an ambulance slowly pulled up next to the cars, and a moment later she heard the sound of the front door opening downstairs.

"Officer?" David said, his voice drifting up from the hallway. "How can I help?"

CHAPTER NINE

"WHAT THE HELL HAPPENED here?" the first paramedic said, leaning into the parked car and peering at Jackie's throat, which had been cut wide open and left with blood oozing down over her chest. "What was used to do this?"

"Look in her right hand," the police officer said.

Looking down, the paramedic saw that Jackie had died holding a very rusty old hacksaw, which had pieces of flesh still attached to the jagged teeth.

"Are you serious?" the paramedic asked as she turned to the officer. "Are you trying to tell me that this woman parked her car and then used that to saw her own throat open? Wouldn't that take... a while?"

"It would to get as deep as she seems to have gone," he replied, "but all the doors were locked when we got here, and so far it's looking like a case of suicide. People can do crazy things when they're not thinking straight, especially if there are any drugs in their system. I wouldn't be surprised to find she was coked up to the eyeballs, something like that. My colleague's just gone to the house down the road to see whether -"

"Jackie?"

Racing out from the driveway, David pushed the officer and then the paramedic out of the way as he dropped to his knees next to the car and looked inside. As soon as he saw Jackie's dead, glassy eyes and the thick wound that had been cut almost all the way through her neck and into her spine, he began shaking her frantically.

"Jackie, talk to me!" he gasped. "Say something! What the hell's going on here? Why are you all just standing around? Do something!"

A short distance away, Mia stepped into view holding Catherine, followed by David. They stood and watched as Nick dissolved into a series of sobs, clinging to his wife's body even as the police officer leaned in and tried to gently pull him away.

"Is that..."

Mia's voice trailed off for a moment, before she turned and stepped back around the corner, holding her hands over Catherine's ears so that she wouldn't be able to hear Nick's anguished cries.

"Sweetheart, it's okay," she whispered. "Don't listen."

"I guess that explains why she left her phone behind," David said, watching as Nick was pulled out of the car, before turning ashen-faced to his wife. "She must have come out here in the night and done this. I just overheard one of the police officers talking on the phone, she seemed pretty sure it was suicide. They're wondering whether she was high on something. I thought she'd kicked all that stuff back in the day, but I suppose it's possible that she relapsed. You didn't see her with anything at dinner, did you?"

"Of course not."

"It all makes sense. She knew we wouldn't approve, so she must've hidden what she was doing."

"I talked to her last night," Mia stammered. "I talked to her right before she went to bed. She was playing with Catherine, she accidentally bumped her against the cupboard but it was nothing."

"The police might want to ask you about that."

"Why?" she replied.

"Just to establish the sequence of events," he explained, before looking back toward the car and seeing that Nick was now on his knees, sobbing in front of the car as the paramedics leaned through the doors and set to work examining Jackie's body. "The last time I saw Jackie was a little before midnight and everything seemed fine. I can't think of anything she said that might have hinted..."

His voice trailed off, and finally he leaned back against the fence and put his hands over his face.

"She was one of my oldest friends," he continued. "If something like this was going on in her mind, why didn't she feel like she could talk to me?"

"You can't blame yourself," Mia told him, putting a hand on the side of his arm. "There's nothing we can do out here. Why don't we head back inside and let them get on with their jobs?"

"I have to check on Nick," he replied, stepping past her and heading back toward the car. "I'll meet you in there!" he called back to her. "I just can't leave Nick right now!"

Left standing alone on the driveway, watching the mass of police officers and paramedics, Mia couldn't help but feel as if she was living in a nightmare, as if she might wake up at any moment. She tried to think of something she could do for David, or for Nick, but she soon realized that if she tried to interfere she'd only get in the way. Turning, she looked back at the house and watched the windows, and for a moment she half-expected to spot someone standing inside and staring back at her. When that failed to happen, she began to make her way back toward the house while gently cradling her daughter.

"We'll make some tea," she said, trying to sound positive for Catherine's sake. "Don't worry about all the flashing lights and scary noises. Let's go inside and sit down, and I'm sure Daddy will be back with us soon."

"Hang on!" David gasped, hurrying past on his way to the front door. "I'd better check Jackie didn't leave any drugs around. If the police want to take a look, the last thing we need is them turning up some bags of coke!"

***

A little under two weeks later, Mia and David stood wearing black as they watched Jackie's coffin being lowered slowly into the ground.

"I guess that's that, then," David whispered. "As funerals go, that was probably one of the slightly less depressing ones I've ever been to."

"I can't believe she's gone," Mia replied, as the coffin disappeared from view. "I also can't believe..."

She paused for a moment, before turning to him.

"Two weeks ago we were planning for a

dinner party and Jackie was texting to make sure we'd got some decent wine in," she continued, "and now she's dead."

"You never know what people are going through," David said, before spotting some familiar figures making their way past. "I know they didn't find any drugs, but I'm still convinced she had to have been up to something. Hang on, that's Jackie's mum and stepdad, I just want to speak to them. Can I meet you back at the car, and then we'll head to the wake?"

"Sure," she replied, but he was already on his way and she was left to turn and start following the others toward the car park.

"Mia?"

Stopping, she turned to find that Nick had hurried over. Slightly red-eyed and clearly struggling after the funeral, he hesitated as if he wasn't quite sure what to say next.

"That was a great reading," she told him.

"Jackie didn't kill herself."

She opened her mouth to reply, but for a moment she wasn't quite sure what to say to him.

"And she wasn't on drugs!" he added. "I know what people are saying, I know all the whispers and rumors, but I'm telling you she was clean!"

"I'm sure she was."

"I know I sound crazy," he continued, "and

I've seen the way people look at me whenever I go on about this, but you were there with us that night. You saw Jackie right before we went to bed. Did she seem like someone who was about to commit suicide?"

"No," Mia replied, "but -"

"Did she seem like someone who was thinking any further ahead than the next drink?" he asked. "No, of course she didn't. She was so excited about all the new projects at work, she was making all these plans. There was a bruise on her head, the coroner said it was probably nothing but I'm trying to get them to take a look at it again. After she died, I got into her laptop and found the proposals she'd written for stuff that's not due to happen until next year. She was full of ideas, she was scheduling so many calls and meetings. Why would she do that if she was planning to..."

His voice trailed off.

"I don't know," Mia said after a moment. "Sometimes people just hide it really well, I guess."

"I know my wife," he said firmly. "Jackie didn't kill herself. The police might not want to listen to me, the rest of the family might think that I'm completely crazy, but no-one's ever going to be able to convince me that the official story makes sense." He took a step back. "I don't know what happened that night. None of us might ever find out. But I promise you one thing... Jackie was killed.

She didn't take that hacksaw and... It's just impossible. I can't believe that she'd ever go out there and sit in the car and do something like that to herself!"

With that, he turned away as other mourners made their way over. Lost in conversation with them, he nevertheless glanced back at Mia until she felt uncomfortable, at which point she turned and began to carry Catherine toward the car park.

"It's okay," she told her daughter, who was starting to seem a little unsettled. "It's just... weird adult stuff. There's nothing for you to worry about."

As they headed to the car park, she heard other mourners talking nearby. Everyone still seemed to be in a state of shock, as if they couldn't believe what they'd been told about Jackie's final moments, and by the time she reached the car Mia worried that somehow the police and the paramedics and all the so-called experts must have missed something. She turned and looked back across the cemetery, and she saw David still taking to Jackie's family, and a shudder passed through her chest as she began to wonder exactly what had happened to Jackie on that fateful night.

In her arms, Catherine gurgled again.

"I know," Mia said, rocking her gently. "Something about this really doesn't feel right to me either."

CHAPTER TEN

"CUCUMBER SANDWICH?"

Startled, Mia looked up and saw a man standing in front of her, holding a plate of sandwiches that he'd evidently collected from the table by the bar.

"They're really good," he continued with a grin. "I should know. I made them myself."

"No, thank you," she replied, trying to sound grateful. "I'm not really hungry."

"Cucumber sandwiches have a bad reputation," the man continued, "but I don't think that's fair at all. In fact, I think they're one of the most amazing snacks anyone can have. They're quick to make, they're cheap, they're filling, they're nutritious, they're even good for the environment. What's not to love? It's about time they came back into fashion. I've actually got my own channel online, promoting them to people all around the world. I'm almost up to fifty followers."

"That's great," Mia replied, glancing past him and looking for David, who'd disappeared around to the far side of the pub's saloon bar a little earlier. "I'm sure you're absolutely right."

"Do you know the history of the cucumber sandwich?" he continued, clearly convinced that he'd finally found a captive audience for his tale. "I've been doing some research and I've produced a series of videos, you can find them if you look for -"

"Excuse me," Mia said, getting to her feet and – still holding Catherine – scooching around the table. "I really need to go and find my husband. Thanks for the offer of the sandwich, though, and I'll be sure to look for your channel."

"I'll catch up to you later!" the man called after her as she headed through to the main bar. "What about your baby? It might like to try a cucumber sandwich! I'll give it one later!"

"Let's hope not," she muttered under her breath, before stopping as she saw the sad sight of Nick slumped in one of the corner booths. "Great," she said to Catherine as she adjusted the baby's position in her arms, "it looks like Uncle Nick's already had a few too many beers. Or spirits. Or both."

Seeing that David was busy talking to some other old college friends, she made her way over to Nick, who was so drunk that he could barely even remain conscious. As she sat next to him, she saw him struggling to open his eyes; he reached out and tried to pick up his glass, which was on the table, but when he saw that it was empty he merely knocked it onto its side.

"Let's put that out of harm's way," Mia said, taking the glass and placing it on another table. "Nick, I think -"

"I keep replaying that night over and over," he said, slurring his words as he pulled his phone from his pocket. He tapped at the screen a few times, launching a video that Mia remembered him filming after dinner at the house. "Look, it's the four of us just sitting around, chatting about all sorts of nonsense." He paused the video on a shot of Jackie's face. "I keep looking for some hint of what's wrong," he continued, "but there's nothing. Look at the woman on that screen, Mia. Does that really look like someone who's planning to kill herself?"

"No," Mia admitted, "it doesn't."

"And does it look like someone who wants to do it in the most hideous way possible?" he asked. "You didn't see her in that car, but I did. She'd cut through almost to the base of her skull. How does anyone even do that? The doctors said it might be possible if she was in some kind of manic state, but I don't buy it. Shouldn't she have passed out much sooner?"

"The car was locked from the inside, wasn't it?" Mia reminded him.

He sighed.

"And the boot too? And the sunroof?"

"I don't care about any of that," he murmured, tapping to start the video again. "That's just a technicality. I'm talking about real human emotions, about the things you can't fake. Things that can't malfunction. But that's what they think happened to Jackie, isn't it? They think she was happy, and that suddenly on that night her emotions malfunctioned and she became sad. They keep hinting at drugs, even though all the toxicology reports came back negative. I was married to her, Mia. I know she wasn't in any kind of mood to kill herself."

"I'm sure you're right," she replied, overwhelmed by sadness as she realized that he really wasn't coping very well at all. She looked around again, hoping that David might show up and save her from an awkward conversation, but there was no sign of him now. "I know you know this, but you can never really understand what's going on in someone's head. I just think that eventually you're going to be able to move past the pain, which is what Jackie would have wanted." She continued to search for David for a moment, before turning to Nick again. "I hope -"

Before she could finish, she saw that he'd nodded off. Realizing that he was way too drunk to talk to anyone, she moved his phone a little further across the table, just to keep it safe in case of any spillages. At the same moment, Catherine began to gurgle, although the gurgle swiftly developed to become the beginning of a full-on crying session.

"Okay, let's pop you outside," Mia said, as she eased herself to her feet. "What's up with you, Catherine? Aren't you enjoying your first funeral?"

***

"Does she seem slightly off to you?" Mia mused a couple of hours later, as David drove them home along the winding countryside lanes. "I don't know, I can't quite put my finger on it, but she's been crying a little more than usual and she just seems... grumpy."

"It's probably gas," he suggested.

"That's your answer for everything," she pointed out.

"And am I wrong?" he asked. "She's a baby, she's got a tiny digestive system, she's bound to have a lot of gas."

"I'm worried it's more than that," she replied, touching the side of Catherine's face, only to set her off crying again. "See? Why's she doing that suddenly? She used to calm down when I touch her, and now it's almost the opposite."

"Do you ever think you're fussing over her too much?"

She turned and glared at him.

"Absolutely not," he continued, clearly recognizing that the suggestion had been a mistake. "It's just baby stuff. We have no idea what's going on in that little head of hers, and frankly it's probably just nonsense anyway. If you want my advice, you'll just leave her alone and let her settle by herself. Otherwise you risk smothering her."

"I'm not going to smother our baby," Mia replied, bristling slightly at the suggestion that she wasn't able to manage the situation properly.

"Did I say the wrong thing?" he asked.

"No."

"I did, didn't I?"

"No!" she said firmly, but she could already feel and hear herself becoming more annoyed. "Let's just leave it, okay? Catherine's been so good up until now, and I don't suppose it really matters if she starts getting a little tetchy. Frankly, she's been almost a miracle baby so far, so I guess she owes us a little trouble." As Catherine's cries became louder, she started rocking the baby gently in her arms. "Mummy's right here," she cooed. "Daddy's here too. You know, I think maybe we shouldn't have taken you to that funeral. I think you picked up some weird vibes from being around so much death and sadness."

She turned to David.

"I think she picked up some weird vibes from being around -"

"I heard you," he replied, and now he was struggling to remain patient as rain began to fall. "Let's just stay positive and not obsess over the tiniest details. A few hours at a funeral won't turn Catherine into some kind of gloomy little monster, and I highly doubt that she's been... absorbing death vibes. The only vibes she's going to absorb are bad vibes from us fussing over her too much." He steered the car around a corner. "I get it, she's your whole life and you don't have anything else to -"

"I'm not smothering her!" she protested.

"Let's not argue in front of her," he added. "That really *might* make her react badly."

"I'm a good mother," she murmured.

"No-one in their right mind could ever argue with that," he told her. "Seriously, Mia, I'm not surprised if this business with Jackie has left you rattled. I know I'm certainly not sleeping too well at the moment, just thinking about that night and wondering whether we could have done anything differently. Whether we could have noticed that she was struggling and maybe stepped in." A few more spots of rain had fallen on the windscreen now, so he switched on the wipers. "I suppose there'll always be that uncertainty. That sense of questioning why we didn't realize she was in such a bad way. And I'm sure it's a thousand times worse for Nick."

"I just feel as if something doesn't quite add up," she told him as Catherine began to cry a little louder. "Come on, there's no need to be upset," she continued, touching the girl's cheek, only to set her off crying even more. "I don't get it, David. It's almost as if Catherine's starting to hate me."

CHAPTER ELEVEN

RAIN WAS POURING DOWN by the time night fell, battering the windows as Mia stopped in the kitchen and peered outside. She watched as drips fell down from the roof, and for a few seconds she felt as if the natural world was trying to blast away any trace of human existence.

"It's really coming down out there," she pointed out, before turning to see that David was still gently rocking Mia in his arms. "At least she's settled now."

"Do you remember Monty?" he asked. "He used to get so freaked out any time there was bad weather. He couldn't handle it at all."

"Yes, but Monty was a dog," she replied, raising a skeptical eyebrow as the lights flickered briefly. "I'm sure you're not comparing our daughter to a German Shepherd."

"I wouldn't dare," he told her, "but -"

Before he could get another word out, the lights went off, plunging the house into darkness. He waited, but after a few seconds he let out a heavy sigh.

"It'll be the fuses," he muttered. "Damn it, that means I'm going to have to go up to the attic, and I'd just managed to get Catherine settled."

"I'll go," Mia replied, opening a nearby drawer and taking out the flashlight, switching it on before casting the beam across the kitchen. "Don't worry, I know how fuse boxes work."

"You just have to trip the -"

"I can do it," she said, picking her way toward the door. "This is the twenty-first century, remember? Women are actually able to perform simple tasks around the house."

"I wasn't being patronizing!" he called after her, but a moment later he heard the sound of her footsteps on the stairs. Sighing, he looked back down at Catherine. "I wasn't!" he protested, before settling her down in her crib. "You know, sometimes I feel like I can't ever do anything right," he continued. "And that's just with your mother. Can you imagine how it's going to be in about a decade and a half, when you hit your teens? There's no hope for me, Catherine. I'm going to be just perpetually wrong all the time!"

***

As soon as she'd unlatched the door to the attic and pulled it open, Mia shone the flashlight up the rickety and narrow wooden staircase that led up into the gloom. She never like the attic even at the best of times, and she was already imagining the hundreds – or maybe even thousands – of spiders that were surely waiting up there.

"I totally should have let David do this," she muttered under her breath, before starting to make her way up. "Why did I have to try to prove some kind of stupid point? And what idiot put the fuses up here, anyway?"

By the time she reached the top of the stairs, she could feel that the air was much colder. She shone the flashlight all around and saw thick rolls of insulation packed into the gaps on the floor, and a moment later when she tilted the beam she flinched as she spotted large cobwebs hanging down from the roof; she couldn't actually see any spiders so far, but she had absolutely no doubt that they were nearby and that they were probably just waiting for a chance to leap down into her hair.

"Let's make a deal, okay?" she said as she began to make her way toward the fuse-box at the far end of the attic. "You won't jump out at me, and in return I won't squash you. Oh, and I'll tell David that he has to get the fuse-box moved to a more convenient location. Why would anyone ever put it in an attic?"

Reaching the box, she opened the panel at the front and saw that – sure enough – one of the switches had been tripped. She pushed it the other way, but she quickly found that it immediately sprang back, as if it simply refused to remain in the correct position.

"Oh, come on," she said with a heavy sigh, "don't make me go all the way back down there and admit that I don't know what I'm doing. He'd have an absolute field day." She tried the switch several more times, only to realize that her luck was out. "That's just the -"

Suddenly she heard a loud bump coming from somewhere nearby. Turning, she shone the flashlight's beam back across the attic, but she saw no sign of anyone.

"David?" she said cautiously. "You didn't come up here to check on me, did you? Because if you did, that might for once be a good idea. I really can't figure this thing out, I think you might need to take a look. And why's the fuse-box in the attic, anyway? Is this really the best place for it?"

She waited for an answer.

"David? Are you up here? You didn't bring Catherine up, did you? It's too cold."

Still waiting, she began to feel a flicker of

concern in her chest. She told herself that a dark and stormy night right after a funeral was *not* the time to start fretting about such things, but she couldn't help worrying that someone else might have caused the strange noise. She continued to shine the beam around for a few more seconds, until she felt sure that there was no sign of anyone else, and then she began to make her way back toward the stairs.

"Great," she said, unable to hide a sense of frustration, "now I have to go back down and admit that I couldn't fix everything after all." She began to carefully pick her way down the stairs. "I'm just -"

In that instant, something slammed hard into her back, knocking her over and sending her tumbling down the steps until she landed with a thud at the bottom. Hitting her head hard, she was immediately knocked unconscious.

***

"Mia, are you okay?" David called out, still sitting in the kitchen with Catherine. He'd heard a heavy bump just a few seconds earlier, coming from the attic, and now the dark house had fallen silent again. "Mia?"

He waited, and then he got to his feet and made his way out into the hall.

"Wait there, Catherine," he said cautiously, reaching out to find the wall and then guiding himself to the bottom of the main staircase. "Mia, are you okay up there?" he continued. "Mia? Can you hear me?"

Unable to shake a sense of concern, he began to make his way up the stairs, worried that his wife might have fallen. By the time he reached the landing, this concern had grown a little, but a moment later – as he started to fumble his way toward the attic door – he heard a shuffling sound coming from somewhere nearby. Turning, he looked into the bedroom and realized he could hear the sound of somebody nearby, so he cautiously headed through the doorway.

"Mia, are you in here?" he asked. "I heard a loud noise."

He stopped and looked at the bed, but there was no sign of his wife. A moment later, however, he felt a hand touching his waist from behind, followed by the sensation of hot breath on the back of his neck.

"Okay, that's good," he replied, starting to turn to her, only for her to hold him firmly in place. "I was worried you'd had an accident," he told her. "What are you -"

Before he could finish, he felt her hand moving down to the front of his shirt, and a moment later she dipped her fingers into his underwear.

"Right now?" he said, unable to stifle a faint smile in the darkness. "Are you serious? We haven't done anything since Catherine was born, and you choose a power cut to make a move?"

Her hand moved further down, until she was touching his crotch directly.

"Catherine's in the kitchen," he continued, aware that this was an inconvenient time but also loathe to turn his wife down after such a long barren spell. "So this is what it takes to get you horny again, is it?" he added. "I've got to admit, Mia, you have an infinite capacity to surprise me. I'd have thought the candles and chocolate would -"

As she gripped his manhood harder, he let out a startled gasp.

"Do you think we could slow down a little?" he asked, but she was already starting to move her hand up and down, caressing him a little more firmly than usual. "I guess we can't," he continued, feeling her pressing her body against him from behind. "Okay, here's the deal, I don't want to be unromantic but I also left Catherine down there in her crib, so I think we should make this a quick one. Do you -"

Suddenly she shoved him hard, pushing him across the room and forcing him onto the bed. Startled, he rolled onto his back and looked up into the darkness as the figure climbed on top of him. She took his hands and forced them onto her chest, and to his surprise he found that she was already naked. Squeezing her breasts, he felt her reaching down to start sliding him inside her body. He couldn't see her face in the darkness, but he told himself that she was probably happy.

"I guess you're taking charge, then," he stammered, unable to hide a sense of shock as she began making love to him in the dark, with rain battering the nearby window. "Well, you know I'm never going to turn that down."

CHAPTER TWELVE

HEARING A DISTANT THUDDING sound, David began to open his eyes. For a few seconds he had no idea where he was, but as he began to sit up he realized that he was on the bed, with the lights off and gentle rain tapping at the window. He blinked a couple of times, wondering what was wrong, and then he heard the thudding sound again, accompanied this time by a voice.

"David?" Mia called out frantically, sounding muffle and far away. "Help me!"

Confused, David stumbled to his feet, only to find that his trousers immediately fell down. Half-remembering the events of a couple of hours earlier, and his wife's very sudden amorous attention, he pulled his trousers up while stepping out of the bedroom and onto the landing. The power was still out, and a moment later he heard Catherine crying downstairs. Now his mind was racing as he tried to piece everything together; he remembered hearing a loud bump upstairs, and then he'd made his way up, only to find that Mia was completely fine and that – in fact – she was feeling frisky. They'd made love for the first time in over a year, and then...

And then what?

"David!" Mia yelled, banging on the inside of the attic door. "Where are you? I'm trapped in here!"

Hurrying to the door, David found that the latch was in place. He pulled it aside and opened the door, only for Mia to immediately tumble out and half-fall against him, gripping his shoulders in an attempt to stay on her feet. She tried to pull away, only to almost fall to the floor; he had to put an arm around her in order to keep her up.

"What the hell happened to you?" he gasped.

"Where's Catherine?" she murmured. "Is she alright? Why's she crying? Why aren't you with her?"

"I just woke up on the bed," he replied, still struggling to understand what was happening as his wife hurried to the top of the stairs. "Mia, do you mind telling me what's going on? Why did you go back up into the attic? What -"

"Get away from my baby!" Mia screamed downstairs, followed by a series of heavy thuds and bumps. "David, help!"

"Mia?" he called out, rushing to the stairs and heading down, as he heard the sound of glass breaking somewhere in the house. "Mia, stop! What are you doing?"

***

"I told you to call the police!" she hissed, cradling the crying Catherine as she stood in the pitch-black kitchen. "David, what's wrong with -"

Before she could finish, the lights flickered back to life. The microwave immediately let out a long beeping sound.

"And what am I supposed to tell them?" David asked, still a little out of breath. "That my wife got spooked by a shadow after hitting her head?"

"I saw someone!" Mia shouted angrily, causing Catherine's cries to become louder. "I'm sorry," she added, kissing the top of the baby's head, "Mummy didn't mean to scare you."

"If I'm going to call anyone," David continued, "it'll be an ambulance. You said it yourself, you fell and got knocked out and then -"

"I didn't fall!" she said firmly. "I was pushed!"

"There's absolutely no sign of an intruder."

"I don't care!" she snapped, before kissing the top of Catherine's head again, trying to calm the baby down. "I don't care, David," she continued, lowering her voice a little, "I know I smacked my head and I know I got knocked out, but that doesn't explain the fact that when I came downstairs just now, a woman was holding our child! She put her in the crib and ran as soon as she realized that I'd seen her, but she was real!"

"Let's rewind a little," David replied. "You went up to the attic to try to fix the fuse-box."

"I already told you that."

"And then you came back down to -"

"And someone pushed me down the stairs! I got knocked out, but they could have killed me!"

"At what point did you get naked?"

"Excuse me?" she replied, her eyes opening wide with shock.

"Wait," he said, putting a hand on the side of his face for a moment as he felt his mind racing, "I'm still confused about the timeline here. You must have gone back up into the attic after we... you know."

"After we *what*?" she snapped.

"You know," he continued, feeling a little helpless. "On the bed?"

"What the hell are you talking about?"

"We had sex," he reminded her. "On the

bed!"

"What?"

"You and me," he added, wondering whether she really might have a serious concussion. "Frankly it's been a long time coming, too. You kind of ambushed me and... well, I'm not going to say you forced yourself on me, because it was certainly welcome. The timing was a little odd but -"

"We didn't have sex!" she spat, as if the idea disgusted her.

"Well, I think you'll find that we did," he told her. "Then I fell asleep, which is something that happens sometimes and -"

"Hang on," she replied, still holding Catherine as she stepped closer to him, "let me get this straight. Are you seriously telling me that after I went into the attic and got attacked, you went into the bedroom and had a nap and then you had some kind of wet dream?"

"No!" he blurted out. "It was you!"

"I was unconscious!"

"You were..." His voice trailed off for a moment as he tried to make sense of everything that was happening. "No," he continued finally, struggling to find the right words, "you came to me, you initiated everything and then we got onto the bed and... did it. Then you must have put your clothes on and gone back to the attic."

"I was unconscious!" she said again, before

hesitating. "Wait, did you have sex with the intruder?"

"No!"

"David -"

"It was you," he said firmly. "I know it was you, Mia. We've been married for long enough now that I know my own wife when I'm making love to her. There are a million little things that you do in bed, things that make you unique, just like everyone has certain... habits. I know your smell, and I know how you kiss, and I know how you react to certain things when we're having sex, and I know what your body feels like. Come on, you can't seriously think that I'd do all of that with someone else and not notice that I've got the wrong person!" He waited for a reply. "Can you?"

"I don't know what to think," she replied, turning and carrying Catherine back across the kitchen, cradling the baby's head gently. "This whole situation is out of control. I think I want to scream."

"All the doors and windows are locked from the inside," he told her. "We've got a state-of-the-art security system. Nobody's broken into the house, Mia, and nobody's been holding Catherine except you and me. I'm not going to claim that I can explain all of this right now, but it's obvious that we've both got our wires crossed. Why don't we just wait until the morning? I'm sure everything will seem clearer in the cold light of day."

"We didn't have sex tonight, David."

"Okay, fine," he continued, choosing not to fight that particular battle. "I'm still worried you might have some kind of concussion."

"I don't," she said, looking out the window as some lingering rain continued to fall. "I feel like I'm losing my mind, though. Sure, I didn't see the woman who was holding Catherine very clearly, but it wasn't a shadow. Shadows don't hold babies up in the air and then set them down, and then run away. Shadows don't make a noise as they race off through the house." She turned to him. "Shadows don't go upstairs and sleep with my husband."

"Fine," he replied, slipping his phone from his pocket, "I'll call the -"

"Don't be stupid," she continued, cutting him off. "It's like you said, they'd never take us seriously. We've got two halves of two very different stories, and they'd probably think we're mad. Hell, they might even be right." She kissed Catherine on the forehead again. "You might have a point. I *did* bang my head pretty hard, and I suppose I could have been confused. It's not a concussion, though. I'm certain of that. So let's just try to go to bed and sleep, and hopefully in the morning things'll get back to normal. I don't know about you, but after the funeral today and everything else that has been happening lately, I feel as if the whole world is turning against me."

"It's not," he told her. "You've got me. And Catherine."

"I know," she continued, forcing a faint smile even though she still felt extremely concerned. "I knew parenthood was going to be crazy, but I never thought it'd be like this. I just want everything to get back to normal." She kissed the top of Catherine's head again. "I want everything to be perfect."

CHAPTER THIRTEEN

"SO CATHERINE'S FAST ASLEEP," David said the following morning, tucking his shirt in as he made his way through from the kitchen, "and the fuse-box seems fine, so I'm just going to pop into town. Will you be okay here by yourself?"

"Why wouldn't I be?" Mia asked, not looking up from the notebook she was reading by the window.

"I just -"

"I'm not some fragile thing," she continued, glancing up at him. "I won't fall apart or start imagining things just because I'm left alone for a few hours. And Catherine will be perfectly safe."

"I never doubted that for a moment," he replied, stopping behind her and leaning down to kiss the top of her head. "You smell great."

"Hmm," she murmured, having already refocused her attention on the notebook.

"You know, we *should* try to be a little more intimate again," he continued, placing his hands on her shoulders. "Regardless of what might or might not have happened last night, I really think -"

"You fell asleep on our bed and had a dream."

"Regardless," he said again, "it's not good for us to... ignore that side of our lives. I love you, Catherine, and I want to explore that love in every way possible. I want to express it and show you what you mean to me."

"Did my package come yet?"

"What package?"

"My new breast pump. Sorry, you talked about expressing and it reminded me." She looked up at him. "The old one still hasn't shown up, by the way. You don't think Jackie would have stolen it, do you? She was obviously pretty screwy that night, so what if she started hiding our stuff? Like you said, she probably wasn't quite thinking straight so she could have gone around moving everything just to freak us out." She thought for a moment. "You can't use a breast pump to take drugs, can you?"

"That seems like quite a reach," he pointed out, before looking at the notebook. "Is that the one I gave you? The one about all the people who lived in this house before us?"

"I just wanted to get an idea of all the people who've called this place home in the past," she said, looking back down at the handwritten text. "Before you start telling me that I shouldn't, I'd like to remind you that you're the one who put this little book together. And so far I haven't found any crazy murderers of people who died in horrifying ways, so there's nothing that stands out as the origin story for a ghost. Think of this as just... historical curiosity."

"I'm starting to wonder whether that book was a good idea," he murmured as he turned and headed toward the hallway. "I'll be an hour or two. Try not to get into too much trouble while I'm gone."

Opening the front door, he began to step outside, only for his foot to bump against a box on the step. Picking it up, he turned it around and saw his wife's name on the label.

"Honey?" he called out. "I think your new pump's here!"

***

"I don't know, Mum," Mia said a short while later, sitting at the kitchen table with the new pump firmly attached to her left breast. "I think I actually *might* be losing my mind after all. I mean, I feel like I'm completely sane, but isn't that how crazy people always feel right before they snap?"

"Is David taking your concerns seriously enough?" Heather replied over the phone. "Mia, he has no right to dismiss your fears. That house is old and there could be all manner of ghostly spirits residing between its walls."

"I don't think -"

"They come out when new families arrive, you know," her mother continued. "They're drawn out from the void of the dead, they have a special curiosity when new living people enter their spaces. It's no surprise if there's a little more activity in the months after you love in. I know you don't like it when I talk about this sort of thing, but you have to remember that I've been researching the paranormal for a number of years."

"David says -"

"David's blind to these things," Heather added. "Darling, you know I like him very much, but the first time I met him I could tell that he was closed off to the world of the spirits. You need to trust your own senses. From what you told me just now, it sounds like you encountered a stage nine ghost last night, and those can leave remarkable physical traces in the real world."

"Okay, now you sound like a lunatic," Mia told her.

"A level nine ghost can be particularly dangerous," Heather explained. "They're usually characterized by the need to correct some kind of injustice that occurred while they were alive. You mentioned a book that David put together for you. Is there any hint in there of someone who might have reason to feel cheated out of something from their mortal days?"

"I don't think so."

"Someone who lost a baby, perhaps?"

"There's nothing like that in there. Not as far as I remember, anyway."

"Do you trust David?" she asked. "Would he perhaps remove anything that you -"

"Mum, now you're getting paranoid," Mia said, cutting her off. "I'm starting to wish I hadn't called you. You're just making me see more and more that this is all in my head. Yesterday was insane, what with Jackie's funeral and the wake, and then the bad weather moved in and I'm still not entirely used to living in the countryside." She looked at the window and saw treetops swaying in the distance. "I'm not completely comfortable with it, to be honest," she added. "I feel like such a useless city-loving moron, but I kind of miss London. Pollution and all."

"You could always tell David that you want to move back."

"No way," she replied. "Moving out here was his dream, and this *is* the perfect house. I'm just being an idiot and staring a gift-horse in the mouth, when I should actually be extremely grateful to David for moving us here. I guess I need to work on keeping my shit together."

"Don't use that sort of language around the baby," her mother said sternly.

"Sorry," Mia replied, before rolling her eyes as she glanced over at Catherine. "If it makes you feel any better, though, I really don't think she's *that* impressionable. Not just yet. She recognizes David and me, and that's about the limit of her cognitive abilities. I sometimes think she -"

Suddenly she heard a heavy thud coming from upstairs. Looking up at the ceiling, she immediately felt her heart starting to race; she told herself to stay calm, but her mind was spinning and she already knew she was going to have to go up and see what was happening.

"Are you okay?" her mother asked.

"Did you hear that?" she replied.

"Hear what?"

"That loud bang. Come on, you must have heard it."

"Darling, I'm sorry, I -"

"I'll call you back," Mia replied, cutting the call and setting her phone down, then getting to her feet. "Catherine, wait here, I'll be -"

Catching herself just in time, she thought back to the sight of her daughter cradled in the arms of a shadowy figure. Illusion or not, she was determined to avoid seeing the same thing twice, so she quickly changed her plans and picked the baby up instead, cradling her gently as she made her way through to the hallway and then headed up the stairs. She was listening out for any hint of another noise, although as she reached the landing she had to admit that the entire house seemed quiet and empty again.

"I'm going round in circles," she whispered, as Catherine let out a brief cry in her arms. "Sweetheart, it's okay, Mummy's just making absolutely sure that there's nothing to worry about."

With each passing second, she felt more and more certain that there was no cause for concern. At the same time, she also knew she couldn't continue to live this way, constantly overreacting to every slight noise and rushing around, terrified all the time that some hidden ghostly figure might be lurking somewhere in the shadows. Feeling as if she wanted to scream, she looked at each of the closed doors in turn before somehow forcing herself to ignore the worst of her fears.

"I'm not going to be this type of woman," she said firmly, partly for her own benefit and partly for any lingering entities that might be listening. "I'm not going to be driven mad by every stupid little noise. Do you understand? I've got enough on my plate raising my daughter, without racing around like this. I'm done."

She waited for a moment, before turning and carrying Catherine back down the stairs.

"It's okay," she continued with a sigh, "Mummy was just talking to herself, but that's all done now. From this moment on, everything's going to go back to normal and we're going to be a happy, sane family. I refuse to get obsessed by things that don't matter!"

CHAPTER FOURTEEN

"HONEY?" DAVID SAID, STANDING in the kitchen and watching as Mia – down on her hands and knees – leaned even further into the cupboard. "What are you doing?"

"I'm trying to find my pump!"

"Didn't your new one arrive?"

"Yes."

"Isn't it any good?"

"It's fine," she continued, throwing some boxes out onto the kitchen floor, "but I want to know where the old one went."

"I'm sure it'll show up," he replied, as he headed to the pram and reached down to tickle Catherine's chin. "Are you really determined to go rooting through everything like this?"

"I have to know!"

"But -"

"Can we just leave it?" she added, sounding increasingly frustrated as she pushed some old tins out onto the floor. "I'm not asking you to help, am I? I just don't like losing things, it's not in my nature and that was a perfectly good breast pump. In fact, it was perfect. The new one's fine, but it doesn't quite have the same suction. That first one was pricey and I hate to think it just vanished from the house."

As Catherine began to cry, David lifted her up from the crib.

"I think you're upsetting our daughter," he told Mia. "I don't think all that clatter -"

He winced as she threw out some more tins, sending them banging loudly against the wall.

"I don't think all that clatter's really doing her much good," he continued, kissing Catherine's forehead and managing to calm her down a little. "Hey, here's an idea, why don't we all go for a nice drive? There's that pub I've been meaning to try a few miles away, I heard they do a really nice lunch."

"No time."

"We'd be a couple of hours at most."

"I said, I don't have time!"

"Is that -"

"I get that this isn't important to you," she continued through gritted teeth, still pulling items out of the cupboard, "but it is to me, so can you please stop nagging? If Catherine seems upset, then by all means take her out of here and get her some fresh air. Take her to the pub, if it's so important to you. Just don't interrupt me when I'm trying really hard to get things in order. It's not respectful."

"Okay," David said, choosing to take the diplomatic approach. "I might just take her out for a little stroll. I don't know where we'll end up, but we'll probably be a few hours. Does that sound good to you?"

He waited for a reply, but he could hear Mia muttering away to himself and finally he realized that she was lost in a world of her own.

"Come on, Catherine," he continued, turning and carrying the girl out of the kitchen. "Looks like it's going to be a Daddy day for you. That's not so bad, is it?"

"You've got to be here somewhere," Mia snapped as she started pulling items from another shelf, sending various tins and boxes skittering across the floor behind her. "I refuse to believe that you vanished!"

***

"And how's my favorite wife?" David asked a few hours later, stepping into the front room and taking a seat next to Mia on the sofa. "Did you find what you were looking for?"

"No," she replied angrily, leafing through the notebook. "That stupid pump must have been... stolen by aliens!"

"These things happen."

She turned and glared at him.

"So are you still reading about the history of the house?" he continued, trying to very quickly change the subject. "How's that going?"

"Look at this," she replied, turning to an earlier section. "You wrote about a woman named Elizabeth Wendell, who lived here in the second half of the nineteenth century."

"I remember," he told her. "She was widowed, and then she lived here alone with a maid."

"There's a little more to it than that," Mia explained. "I did some research online, and I bought another membership to that family tree app, and I discovered a lot more about Elizabeth Wendell and her supposed maid. For example, did you know that the maid was named Gretchen Forke, and she was only about ten years younger than her mistress?"

"Okay, but how does -"

"Both women were childless," she continued, speaking so fast now that she almost tripped over her words. "In both cases, the 1841 and 1851 census records show them living in different parts of the country, married and with children, but they both lost those children. Then by the 1881 census Gretchen was widowed and living here as a maid. The similarities between their lives are remarkable."

"I guess that gave them something to talk about," David pointed out.

"There were rumors, too, that they were more than just friends," Mia told him. "Obviously it's impossible to be sure, but apparently a lot of the locals thought that Elizabeth and Gretchen lived out here as a couple."

"Oh, right," David said, raising both eyebrows at once. "Well, that's very forward-thinking of them. These days, no-one would -"

"Whatever entity is haunting this house," she added, "it's focused on Catherine. You must have noticed that. What if one of these two dead women is still here, and she's somehow trying to become in death the mother she could never be in life?"

"That's a bit of a stretch."

"The pieces all fit," she replied. "I don't know which one of them it could be, or if it might even be both of them, but something seems to be fixated on our daughter. We can't let Catherine out of our sight while I'm continuing with my research, but I'm going to sign up to some other apps and see if they have any more information."

"Hold up," he said, "how much is that going

to cost?"

"As much as it takes," she said firmly. "Our daughter's safety might be at risk. Plus, some of my research has uncovered another odd fact. In the 1911 census, there was someone else living here, a young girl named Primrose who was only ten years old. Do you realize what that means?"

"One of the women... got herself pregnant somehow?"

"Possibly. Or they might have stolen themselves a child. The 1921 census only came out recently, you have to wait a hundred years to access this stuff, but by that point no-one was living here. They were all gone, and there's no trace of Primrose in any records at all. I even checked emigration lists, and there's no sign of her. Do you realize what that means?"

"It could mean a lot of things."

"It means something nefarious might have happened to them," she continued, raising her voice a little. "It means there's a gap in the story, and I think that gap might explain what's been happening to us over the past few weeks. Any one of those three people who lived here might have had a good reason to covet a child, and now we've brought a child into the house! Do you realize what that means?"

"You need to up your dosage?"

"Why are you patronizing me?" she shouted

angrily, almost shaking with rage. "I know what I saw! I played it down because I was scared of your reaction, but I know I saw someone holding our daughter! And before you tell me yet again that there's no way anyone could have got into the house, I know that too!"

David opened his mouth to reply, before turning and heading to the door.

"Where are you going?" she called after him.

"Out!" he yelled back at her. "I'm sorry, Mia, but I've just about had enough of your histrionics and paranoia! I'm going to the pub and I'll be back when I've calmed down, and when I can trust myself not to say anything I'll regret."

"You're leaving?" she stammered, hurrying after him, reaching the hallway just in time to see him stepping outside. "David, we're in the middle of an argument!"

"I can't talk to you when you're like this," he replied, turning to her as Caroline began to cry in the other room. "You get so caught up in all this nonsense that you can't see what's really going on, and then you try to drag me into it, but I'm not going to let that happen this time! We have so much going for us now, Mia, and all I need you to do is keep your head together! While I'm out, can you just try to work out what's most important to you? Because I won't let you ruin our future!"

With that he slammed the front door shut, leaving a stunned Mia standing alone in the hallway, listening to the sound of her daughter crying. A moment later that sound was joined by another, as David drove away at full speed along the pebble-covered driveway.

CHAPTER FIFTEEN

"HEY THERE," MIA SAID, sniffing back tears as she sat by the crib in the front room and watched Catherine sleeping, "I'm sorry about earlier. It's not your fault you've got a mummy who..."

Her voice trailed off for a moment as she tried to work out how to sum up her problems in one easy sentence.

"Well, I've had a few wobbles in the past," she continued. "Nothing major, but I've had to take some medicine now and again." Reaching into the crib, she gently stroked the side of her daughter's face. "The thing is, I'm completely better now," she explained. "Daddy's just hyper-sensitive about it, and he overreacts a little bit, but that doesn't make him a bad person. Far from it, actually. He just cares too much."

Smiling through the tears, she wondered how one baby could be so utterly perfect.

"But I'll be stronger," she added. "This is all my fault, and I've fixed it before so I'll fix it again. And it'll be easier this time, because I've got you, and you're all that matters to me in this whole -"

Before she could finish, she heard a bump coming from upstairs. She flinched and visibly tensed, but after a moment she let out a long, slow breath.

"See?" she continued. "I'm not going to let that affect me. I could easily get up and start storming around, calling out to some imaginary presence, but I simply refuse. I've learned from my past mistakes and -"

She flinched as she heard the sound of a door creaking somewhere far off in the house, but again she managed to stay seated next to the crib.

"That's just the wind," she told Catherine. "This is an old house, and although Daddy made a lot of repairs, I'm sure there are still some gaps here and there. I'll get him to oil the doors in the morning. Or I could do it myself! I don't think I'm so helpless that I can't oil a few hinges." She adjusted Catherine's woolly cap a little. "And Mummy and Daddy won't fight again," she added softly. "I promise. I'll make it all up to Daddy when he gets home, and then -"

Suddenly the lights flickered off, plunging

the entire house into darkness.

"Are you kidding me?" Mia said with a sigh, looking up at the ceiling. "I really don't want to go poking about in that attic again. Hopefully it's just a short power cut and everything'll be fine in a moment." She waited as the seconds ticked past. "Any time now," she added. "The power's going to come back on and -"

In that instant, she heard footsteps marching across one of the rooms upstairs. Unable to hide her fear any longer, she got to her feet and looked over at the door that led out into the hallway, and the footsteps continued for a couple more seconds until they seemed to stop at the top of the stairs.

"It's nothing," Mia whispered, even as her voice began to tremble with fear. "It's just..."

She took a deep breath, trying to calm herself down, and then she slowly reached into the crib and picked her daughter up, trying not to wake her in the process.

"Just stay quiet," she continued, "and -"

Suddenly she heard footsteps moving slowly down the stairs. From where she was standing, she couldn't see the bottom of the staircase, but she was sure now that somebody was walking down from the house's upper floor. She waited, holding her child and holding her breath, until finally she spotted a shadow moving across the hallway's far wall.

"Who's there?" she called out as the shadow slipped out of view. "Who are you? What do you want?"

Again she waited, still clutching Catherine, but now she could hear the footsteps moving into the kitchen. She slowly turned and looked at the other doorway, before taking a couple of steps back. She knew that David hadn't returned, that he couldn't possibly have made it back into the house without her having heard, so she took a couple more steps and prepared to run. She told herself that she could get to the front door and then race out along the driveway, and that no-one would be able to catch her. Finally, with the house having returned to silence, she began to edge herself toward the door that led into the hall.

In her arms, Catherine let out a very faint cry.

"Try to stay quiet," she whispered. "I need you to be brave, Catherine. Just for a few more minutes."

Reaching the doorway, she looked at the stairs and saw that there was no sign of anyone. She took a step to the side, and then she froze as she realized she could see something sitting on the kitchen counter. Staring through at that room, she squinted slightly, only to finally realize what she was seeing.

"My pump," she said softly, realizing that

this was the breast pump she'd lost, the same one she'd been trying to find for so long. "What the..."

She swallowed hard, but she knew deep down that she shouldn't go and take a look. After all, the pump's sudden reappearance seemed like some kind of freaky dare, as if someone was trying to tempt her to go through to the kitchen. Instead, she began to back toward the front door, while trying to work out where to go once she managed to get outside. She told herself that she'd have to go left at the end of the driveway and then hope to get all the way to the nearest village, although there was always a chance she might be able to flag down a passing motorist.

Slowly she reached behind, trying to find the door's handle in the darkness.

At that moment, a female figure walked calmly past the kitchen door, appearing for a few seconds before stepping out of sight again.

In Mia's arms, Catherine began to wake up, letting out a series of spluttering gurgles.

"It's okay," Mia whispered, finding the handle and trying to give it a turn, only to find that it was firmly locked. "Sweetheart, we're getting out of here. I don't know what's going on right now, but we can figure it out after Daddy comes home. And with the police here."

She tried the handle a couple more times, before turning and trying to work out why the damn thing refused to open. Once she was sure that the handle wasn't going to turn, she began to search for a key, only to spin back around as she heard a scraping sound coming from somewhere nearby.

"Who's there?" she shouted, unable to hide a sense of panic. "Get away from us!"

She continued to pull on the door, but at the same time she was trying to figure out how else she might be able to get out of the house. She knew the windows used toughened glass and that breaking out would be practically impossible, but she figured that the back door might well be unlocked. Besides, a spare set of keys sat in a bowl next to the kitchen table, so after a few seconds she realized that this would be her best chance.

"Okay, Catherine," she said quietly, "I'm going to have to run, so just stay calm. We're going in three, two..."

Racing forward, she hurried through the doorway and into the kitchen. Barreling to the back door, she tried to pull it open, only to find that this too was locked. She tried over and over, convinced that she couldn't possibly be locked inside her own home, but seconds later she spun round as she heard something bumping against the sideboard.

Hurrying to the counter, she grabbed one of the largest knives and held it up, while looking around the darkened kitchen and trying to spot the intruder.

"I'm armed!" she called out, frustrated by her own inability to hide the sheer terror that was filling her voice. "Do you hear me? I've got a knife and I'm not afraid to use it!"

Watching the shadows, she told herself that at any moment some kind of terrifying figure was about to appear. After a few seconds she spotted the breast pump again, still sitting on the counter, and she couldn't help but wonder why anyone would want to hide such a thing; a moment later, spotting something on the floor, she looked down and saw that the newer pump had been smashed to pieces.

"This doesn't make any sense," she told herself, before remembering that the keys in the bowl might yet allow her to get the door open.

Stepping forward, still holding the knife, she made her way to the bowl and began to sort through the various sets of keys. Finding the set she needed, she hurried to the back door, only to fumble as she tried to sort through the keys; the set fell to the floor, and Mia let out a few muttered curse words as she reached down and grabbed them, before struggling to fit them into the lock.

"It's okay," she told Catherine, "I'm not -"

Before she could finish, she saw her own reflection in the door's black glass, and to her horror she realized that the silhouetted figure of another woman was standing right behind her. Still brandishing the knife, Mia turned and held the knife up, and in that moment she saw the intruder's face. She could only scream.

CHAPTER SIXTEEN

AS HE SWITCHED THE engine off, David leaned back in his seat and sighed. During the drive home, he'd felt an increasingly tight knot of dread in his chest, and now as he stared at the house he found himself wondering whether Mia would still be in such a hysterical state.

He knew he shouldn't have stormed out of the house a few hours earlier, but deep down he also knew that he'd been trying to deescalate the entire situation. For so long now he'd believed that Mia was over the worst of her troubles, but recently a few doubts had begun to creep into his mind. Even now, as he forced himself to climb wearily out of the car, he caught himself wondering whether he should call his wife's doctor and suggest an increase in her dosage. And as he unlocked the front door of the house and stepping inside, he wondered whether or not he should feel guilty for seeking out a chemical solution.

Taking a deep breath, he realized that he had no idea what to expect. Would she have calmed down, would she still be angry, or might she have slipped completely over the edge?

After hanging his jacket on the hook, he looked across the brightly-lit hallway and realized that the house seemed completely silent. He waited, but now the silence seemed strangely unnerving. He'd imagined all sorts of possibilities, but all of them had involved some obvious sign of Mia's presence.

"Honey?" he called out. "Mia? I'm back!"

He waited.

Silence.

"In here," she replied suddenly, raising her voice just high enough for him to hear.

Making his way through to the kitchen, he prepared himself for a confrontation, although this time he'd already decided to just bite his tongue and opt for peace over being right. Reaching the doorway, he stopped and looked through, and in that instant he felt a flicker of surprise as he saw his wife. Of all the possibilities that had crossed his mind, this was not one of them.

"Mia?"

***

"Sshhh," Mia Rush purred, as she sat feeding Catherine directly, without using a bottle this time. "Don't make too much noise. She's already almost too sleepy to feed."

"How are my two favorite girls doing?" he asked cautiously, making his way over to the counter before reminding himself that Mia never liked being referred to as a 'girl'. "Sorry, I mean -"

"We're fine," she replied, looking up at him with a smile that seemed just a little forced. "Why wouldn't we be? Everything's completely okay here. After all, what could be more natural than a mother feeding her beautiful, bouncing little baby girl?"

"If -"

"We've just been having some quiet time, that's all," she continued, interrupting him again. "Did you have a nice time at the pub? Was it busy down there?"

"It was fine," he told her. "I only had one drink, because I was driving. I drank it very slowly." He watched her for a moment longer, still puzzled by her calm demeanor. He'd been expecting to walk in and find that he was still in trouble, yet for some reason his wife seemed to have dropped all her anger. The one thing he hadn't been expecting, he realized, was normality. "I wasn't gone for that long, was I? A couple of hours?"

"Well, we've been just fine here," Mia said with a smile. "Actually, that's not quite true, I have to admit that I had a slight wobble after you left. I thought I heard something, and the power went out briefly, but it's all under control now."

"It is?"

"Of course," she continued. "Sorry, I'd get up and make you a drink, but I don't really want to disturb Catherine. She's such a sweet and well-behaved baby, isn't she? Sometimes I wonder how she can be so perfect." She looked down and watched for a few seconds as the baby continued to feed; she adjusted her hold, trying to make it a little easier for the girl. "But she *is* perfect," she added. "She's perfect in every single possible way. Sometimes I think I could just sit and stare at her forever."

"So are you still worried about..."

As his voice trailed off, Mia looked up at him again.

"You know," he said awkwardly, "the... stuff?"

"Stuff?"

"The notebook," he reminded her. "I don't mean to dig it up, but earlier you were really fussing about those people who used to live here. Something about some women and their children. Or lack thereof. Are you still worried about that?"

"It's easy to get caught up in that sort of

thing," she told him. "I know better than most people just how tempting it can be to fall for... crazy suggestions. I'm truly sorry that I let my fears get on top of me, but I want you to understand that I'm completely over it now. I thought it all through, I applied logic and rational reasoning to the situation, and I came to the understanding that I was seeing patterns where there were none. You're completely right, no matter what might have happened here a long time ago, there's really no such things as ghosts."

"Seriously?" He stared at her, barely able to believe that those words had come from his wife's mouth. "You don't believe in ghosts at all now?"

"Why should I?" she asked, getting to her feet with a smile, before heading to the crib and settling her daughter back down. "The people who lived here in the past might very well have lived terrible, tragic lives, but those lives ended when they died. The idea that some part of their souls might be lingering, that they're still here and they're haunting us, is just ludicrous. It's like some kind of silly science-fiction idea that couldn't possibly happen in real life."

"Science-fiction?"

"Or horror," she added. "Whatever."

She took a moment to adjust the blanket in the crib, before making her way over to her husband and placing one hand on his chest.

"I'm really sorry I put you through all of that," she told him. "I'd never intentionally do anything to make you worry. You mean the world to me, all the worlds, and I only want to make you happy. I hope you realize that. You're so handsome."

"Sure," he said cautiously, "but... I'm still not sure what brought about this sudden change."

Reaching out, she touched the side of his head for a moment, tousling his hair as if she couldn't quite believe that she was seeing him at all. Tears began to show in her eyes, but she quickly smiled them away.

"Think of it as a sudden conversion," she told him, before biting her bottom lip for a moment. "Speaking of sudden conversions, why don't we leave Catherine down here for half an hour or so, while we pop upstairs? She's exhausted and she'll be sleepy after her feed, and I think it's been way too long since we properly spent some intimate time together. You've been so busy with your work."

"I have?"

"Probably. I assume. You know what I mean."

"Are you suggesting..."

His voice trailed off for a moment, before a slow smile began to spread across his lips as she reached down and gripped the front of his trousers.

"I have so much," she whispered softly, "to apologize to you for."

"You do?"

"More than you can possibly know."

"I've got to admit," he said cautiously, "I'm starting to really like this new side of you, Mia. I always knew things would get back to normal after you'd had the baby, and I suppose despite my earlier frustrations this is right on schedule." He placed a hand on one side of her waist. "I've missed you, you know."

"And I've missed you," she said softly. "In fact, you have no idea how much. That's why I want us to start reconnecting a little, just to make sure that our bond is as strong as it used to be. You can't possibly begin to imagine how important that is for me."

"I'm sure it is," he told her, "but I certainly don't mind proving the fact."

"I just need to get myself ready," she replied. "Why don't we meet upstairs in the bedroom in ten minutes? And David, I just hope you realize how much I -"

Suddenly she turned and looked across the hallway, as if spooked by something. When David followed her gaze, he realized that she seemed to be looking at the door to the front room, although he had no idea what might have attracted her attention.

"Mia?" he said after a few more seconds had passed, worried that her fears of the paranormal might have returned. "Did you hear something?"

He waited, and after a moment she turned to him again.

"No," she stammered, although she still seemed a little troubled. "Why? Did you?"

"No," he replied, "but I'm not the one who's been getting spooked in the house recently."

"I didn't hear a thing," she told him, not entirely convincingly, as she took a step back. "I'll just pop to the downstairs bathroom and I'll be up in ten minutes. I want to be my best for you, that's all."

"I'll see you up there," he replied, turning and heading up the stairs. "Don't leave me waiting too long! You know how quickly I can get ready for something like this. I don't want you to keep teasing me!"

"I won't," she said with a smile. "You really don't have to worry. I've been waiting for tonight just as long as you have. Maybe even longer."

Once she was alone, Mia looked again at the door to the living room. She glanced up the stairs to make sure that her husband was out of sight, and then she hurried to the door; looking into the room, she saw no sign of anything untoward, although she still hesitated for a moment before reaching over and switching off the light, plunging the room into darkness. She watched the shadows, and then she turned and headed toward the stairs.

Shrouded in darkness now, the living room remained completely still and silent. The window rattled slightly as as a cold wind blew outside, but otherwise the room was quiet, with no signs of life whatsoever. Most of the carpet looked entirely undisturbed.

CHAPTER SEVENTEEN

"HEY," DAVID SAID THE following morning as he wandered bleary-eyed from the hallway and stopped to look across the kitchen. "What smells so -"

Before he could finish, he saw something he hadn't seen in a very long time: Mia was cooking, managing several pans at once while also dealing with something in the oven and some toast set out on two plates. For a few seconds, David could only watch as she moved quickly from one task to the next, getting things done at lightning speed as the smell of frying eggs and bacon filled the room. She appeared to be nothing less than a multi-tasking domestic goddess.

"Am I still asleep?" he asked cautiously. "Is this all a dream?"

"Take a seat," she replied, "breakfast's almost ready."

"Breakfast's usually some cereal and milk," he pointed out cautiously, "and that's on a good day."

"I'm fully aware," she continued, "that I haven't perhaps been the perfect wife lately. Believe me, I recognize the signs. It's not hard to see when a man isn't being supported at home, you can always see it in his eyes." She turned and smiled at him. "You work hard and you need my full support. I get that. We're a team and I need to pull my weight properly."

"Are you trying to fatten me up for something?" he asked as he headed to the table and looked down to see Catherine sleeping happily in her crib. "Is -"

"She's been fed and she's fine," Mia told him. "Today's your day off, isn't it? I want you to have the most relaxing day possible, so that you're all fired up for when you get back to things tomorrow."

"That's... very nice of you," he replied.

"Last night we reconnected," she continued. "Several times, in fact. You've got to admit, it felt good, right?"

"It felt amazing," he said with a faint smile. "To be honest, I'm still feeling a little tired. But you don't have to go to all this trouble, Mia. I don't want you wearing yourself out."

"Cooking breakfast is the least I can do," she explained. "I don't know what you've got planned for the rest of the day, but Catherine and I are here and ready if you fancy spending time together. Or if you'd rather get on with some personal projects alone, that's fine too, I can take Catherine out for a stroll in her pram and let you have the entire house to yourself. All you have to do is tell me exactly what you'd prefer."

"Who are you and what have you done with the real Mia?" he joked, before rubbing the back of his neck. "I think I want to do a little painting, but then this afternoon we could go for a walk. If we head down to the river, we could make it all the way to that little pub by the lock, and then if we time it right we could think about eating dinner there. I can even go online and book a table."

"I'd love that," she said as she began to serve up the cooked breakfast. "In fact, I can't possibly imagine anything more perfect."

***

"Daddy's working right now," Mia purred a few hours later, as she leaned down into the crib and watched Catherine's smiling face for a moment. "We're going out later, though. Doesn't that sound great?"

In response, Catherine offered a brief laugh.

"You're so wonderful," Mia continued, reaching in and stroking the baby's shoulder. "You realize that, right? It's hard to believe that something so perfect could come out of -"

She caught herself just in time.

"Well, it's just so crazy that two people can create life like this," she added softly. "Your daddy would be so proud if he could see you right now, snuggling in your crib and barely even crying. You're so well-behaved, aren't you?" She paused for a few more seconds. "And you fed so well last night," she continued, as tears once again began to fill her eyes. "Aren't human bodies the most wonderful things? It's as if both of us just... knew, somehow."

Catherine laughed again, but at that moment Mia heard a phone ringing nearby. Glancing across the room, she saw the phone flashing on the kitchen table; she made her way over and swiped to unlock the screen; the sensor displayed an error message, claiming that her thumbprint was incorrect. She tried again, and this time – after a moment's consideration – the phone unlocked for her and she saw Nick's name flashing. She looked at her thumb briefly, marveling at the print, and then she glanced at the phone again.

"What do *you* want?" she murmured, hesitating for a few more seconds before answering the call. "Hey, Nick, long time no -"

"I'm going to send you a video," he replied, sounding completely frazzled and anxious. "I'm sending it through right now."

"What are you -"

"I'm sending it to you rather than David because I figure you'll be more open to this sort of thing," he continued. "Did you get it yet?"

"Hang on," she replied, checking her messages and seeing that a video file was on the way, although it was taking a while to load. "It's almost here, but what -"

"As soon as it's ready, you have to watch it," he continued, interrupting her yet again. "I ran it through some programs that enhance certain things. I'd been watching it a lot and I knew something was off, but I just couldn't quite figure out what. It's like deep down, my senses were trying to tell me something but I had to really dig around so that my eyes could catch up. The file I've sent you is from that night Jackie and I spent at your place, right before... Well, you know when I'm talking about."

"Okay, but -"

"Is it there yet?"

"Not quite," she replied, seeing that the video still hadn't quite loaded. "It must be quite a big file. Hey, when -"

"You'll understand everything when you see it," he said firmly, just as the video finished loading.

"I mean, you'll understand why I'm freaking out, at least. The rest, I'm not so sure, I still can't quite wrap my head around it or around what this means for what happened to Jackie, but can you just watch it?"

"Sure," she said, tapping to start the video, furrowing her brow as she saw David laughing and holding a bottle of wine as music played in the background. "Is this -"

"So this is the night when Jackie died," Nick said, "and everyone's having a great time, right? I'm sure you remember, we were maybe slightly tipsy, at least some of us. We were at the dining table and I was filming, like I always do, and like Jackie always hates."

Mia watched as her own face came onto the screen, followed a moment later by Jackie's beaming grin.

"Fast forward to about one minute in," Nick continued. "Sorry, I should have trimmed it down before I sent it to you, but I didn't think. I'm kind of freaking out here right now."

Mia swiped to move to the one minute mark, and she saw that the video was showing more of the same.

"Watch the door behind David's head," Nick said firmly. "You see the door leading to the hallway? With the lights off in there?"

"Yes," she said cautiously, "but -"

"Just freeze it when that's in shot."

She tapped to pause the video, and in that moment she began to realize what he meant. Zooming in slightly, she saw that a figure was standing in the hallway; although this figure was difficult to make out in the darkness, she could just about tell that it was a woman, and she felt a shudder pass through her chest as she realized that she'd seen this woman before. Many times.

"There was someone else in the house that night," Nick continued. "Do you get it now? I've been trying to understand why Jackie suddenly would have done what she did, but this proves there was someone else there. You, me, David and Jackie are all in the video, so who the hell is that watching us from the hallway?"

"I don't know," Mia replied through gritted teeth, unable to stop staring at the grainy image of the woman.

"But you see her, right?" Nick said. "Tell me you see her! Damn it, I have to go to the police with this, it changes everything! If there was someone else lurking in the house like some kind of ghost, then that means Jackie might not have killed herself! Hell, it proves that she didn't!"

"I..."

Mia paused for a few seconds, squinting slightly but still not able to make out any more details of the woman's features.

"The police probably have way better programs for this sort of thing," Nick continued. "They can probably extract her face somehow from the video and then try to identify her. I mean, they have to do something, don't they?"

"I..."

Mia swallowed hard. Her mind was racing and she knew she had to act fast.

"I don't see anyone," she said finally.

"What?"

"I don't see anyone, Nick," she continued, still staring at the figure. "I'm sorry, I see a blur and maybe some noise, some digital artifacts from whatever program you've used, but that program could easily have introduced all sorts of things. Trying to claim that this set of shapes somehow looks like a person... I'm sorry, but you're really reaching here, and I just think you need to calm down and take a break."

"There's someone in the video!" he said angrily.

"You're embarrassing yourself, Nick," she replied. "Have you been drinking? If you go to the police with this, they're going to laugh at you and say you're crazy."

"She's right there!"

"I'm sorry," she continued, "I'm very busy and I don't have time for this. My advice would be for you to cut back on the booze, take some time away from your computer, and try to find something positive to occupy your time with. Fixating on a bunch of conspiracy theories is never going to bring you happiness. You understand that, right? What do you think Jackie would want you to be doing right now?"

She waited, but for a moment she heard no reply at all.

"Conspiracy theories?" he said finally, sounding as if he genuinely couldn't believe what he'd just heard. "Are you serious? Look at the picture in the video! It's right there!"

"I'm going to hang up now, Nick," she replied. "For your own good. Try to get some rest."

"When -"

After cutting the call, she stared at the image in the video for a moment longer. Another shiver ran through her bones, but after a few more seconds she heard Catherine letting out a faint gurgle. She took a moment to delete the video, and then she set the phone back down before making her way over to the crib.

"There's no need to grumble," she said as she lifted Catherine up into her arms. "That was nothing to worry about. I've got a feeling we're going to have a really nice day today. Now that we're finally together."

CHAPTER EIGHTEEN

"AND ONE LEMONADE FOR you," David said a few hours later, as he set a pint glass on the table in the pub's beer garden, overlooking a river that ran gently through the village. "You know, you *could* have had a beer."

"It's so similar," she replied, watching as some swans made their way past, "but there are just one or two tiny differences."

"Huh?"

Shaking herself out of her daydream, she turned to him.

"Thanks," she said with a smile, before taking a sip from the lemonade. "I really needed this."

"So are you teetotal now?" he continued, before enjoying a sip of beer. "Is this a breast milk thing still? Are you worried that if you have a beer, Catherine'll get drunk next time she latches on? Because I really don't think that's how it works." He thought for a few seconds. "Is it?"

"I'm just trying to be a little healthier these days," she told him. "I'm not saying that there's anything wrong with a drink, though. You really deserve that pint."

"I must admit, I agree with you," he said, as his phone buzzed and he pulled it from his pocket. "I'm glad you're feeding directly again, too. Damn it, Nick's trying to get through, I had a missed call from him earlier and -"

"Don't answer it!" she said firmly.

He looked over at her.

"He called me earlier too," she continued, choosing her words with great care, "and to say he was drunk would be a massive understatement. I don't think he's taking things too well, and he was ranting and rambling and frankly saying some pretty offensive things."

"He was?"

The phone in his hands was still ringing.

"I just don't think you should answer it right now," she told him. "It'd only encourage him, and he really needs to get some sleep and dry out. I'm sure he has people in London who are keeping an eye on him. He has a support system, and there's no need to answer the phone and risk fueling whatever paranoia he's experiencing. You'd probably only make things a thousand times worse."

"I'm sure you're right," David said as the ringing sound cut out. "Well, that's taken the decision out of my hands, hasn't it?" He set the phone back down. "I'll call him back in a day or two. I know what Nick gets like when he's drunk, he can be a total pain in the backside. If I say I don't want to have to deal with him right now, does that make me a bad person?"

"Not at all," she replied, unable to hide a sense of relief. "You know, sometimes I wish the rest of the world would just go away and leave us alone. We don't need them, right? Not after everything we've been through to reach this point."

"That's a little extreme," he said cautiously. "I think it's probably good to have the rest of the world out there. Just for when it's needed, you know?"

She opened her mouth to disagree, but at the last second she held back for a few seconds as if she understood now that she'd perhaps jumped the gun a little.

"I'm sure you're right," she told him. "Sorry, that was just me thinking out loud for a moment when I really don't need to." She reached over and grabbed one of the menus, making a point of examining the list of mains. "I don't know about you, but after that walk I'm absolutely famished.

Have you heard anything about what the steaks are like here?"

***

By the time they got home, Mia felt absolutely exhausted, and as she settled Catherine down to sleep she couldn't help glancing at the clock on the wall and wondering how early would be too early to go to bed herself.

"Mummy's had a *very* hectic twenty-four hours," she murmured. "I think I'm still not quite settled. You wouldn't believe some of the -"

Stopping herself just in time, she glanced at the open door, but a moment later she heard David coughing downstairs. In the background, the latest episode of *Midsomer Murders* was still running.

"None of that matters now," she continued, looking back down at the baby. "The past is the past, and the present is the present, and more importantly of all the future is the future. And here... is here. I have to remember that, and I have to focus on it. What happened last night was just an... aberration..."

For a moment she couldn't help but think back to the events of the previous night, but she quickly forced those thoughts from her mind. Somehow certain images tried to force their way back in, as if her part of her own head was acting against her, and she had to really focus in an attempt to stay focused on the here and now.

"I beat it," she whispered in an increasingly desperate attempt to remain calm. "I stopped the -"

Suddenly worried that she was being watched, she turned and looked toward the open doorway. She could see no-one, yet she felt her heart racing and she couldn't shake the fear that at any moment a figure might jump out at her. The paranoia was taking root in her heart and stretching its tendrils throughout her body, even though she'd already told herself so many times that she needed to maintain complete control.

"You can do this," she said firmly. "After everything you went through..."

"Mia," David said suddenly, "I don't think we should do this. It's wrong on so many levels."

"What?"

Startled, she turned to look back across the room. Her heart was racing, but she let out a sigh of relief as she saw that there was no sign of David at all; he coughed again downstairs as the sound of the television continued, and she told herself that his voice had just been an echo in her mind.

Hearing Catherine starting to cry, she turned and looked down at the child. Picking her up from the crib, she pulled her close against her chest and began to rock her gently back to sleep.

"It's okay," she said softly, "Mummy's here.

You know that, right? There's absolutely no reason in the whole wide world why you should be scared."

She waited, but Catherine was crying a little louder than before, as if she was troubled by something.

"Mummy's right here," Mia continued, struggling to stay calm as a shiver passed through her chest. The child was crying loudly now and had begun to wriggle, as if she was trying to get free. "Don't do that," Mia muttered under her breath. "Why are you behaving like this? All I'm doing is trying to be nice to you? I'm holding you and I'm loving you, I'm even feeding you from my own body. Do you understand what a miracle that is, and what it means? Why are you rejecting me?"

She leaned closer.

"Catherine, I -"

Before she could finish, Catherine reached out with her left hand, scratching her nails against Mia's face. Letting out a shocked gasp, Mia dropped the child into the crib and pulled back, before reaching up and touching the marks on her cheek; when she checked her fingertips, she saw that she was bleeding a little, with blood smeared across the prints on the ends of her fingers.

"Why the hell did you do that?" she snapped angrily, storming back to the crib and reaching down to grab the girl again, before stopping at the very last second. "I -"

In that instant, she realized that all her anger and fury was misplaced, and that she should never even think of taking her own problems out on her daughter. Shocked by her own reaction, she placed her hands on the sides of the crib and tried to pull herself together.

"Mia?" David called up from downstairs. "Is everything okay?"

"Everything's fine!"

"I thought I heard -"

"I told you, everything 's fine!" she snapped angrily as Catherine continued to cry. "She's just being a little pain, but I'm sure it's nothing. I'll be down soon." She waited for an answer. "It's probably just gas."

"If you're sure."

"I'm sure," she said under her breath as she heard him walking back through to the front room.

After a few seconds, with Catherine still crying, she realized that she needed to calm her racing mind. She took a series of deep breaths, reminding herself that she wanted to be the perfect mother, and then she very gently reached back into the crib and lifted Catherine out again. This time, even though the child's cries were making her shudder as if somebody nearby had run their fingernails down a chalkboard, she forced herself to simply hold Catherine closer and rock her gently in an attempt to get her back to sleep.

"Hush," she cooed, "it's alright. Mummy's right here, and she's never going anywhere. She -"

Looking at the doorway again, she felt for a moment as if someone had been out there. She watched the landing, terrified that at any moment a figure might appear, and for a few seconds she entirely forgot to rock her daughter.

"You're not there," she whispered. "I know you're not. You can't be. You're gone and you're never..."

Her voice trailed off for a few seconds as she continued to watch the door, and as Catherine continued to cry loudly in her arms.

"You're gone," she added finally, as a shudder of dread passed through her chest and she remembered her encounter in the kitchen during the night, "and you're never, ever coming back."

As she continued to gently rock Catherine, she failed to notice that she'd left one bloodied fingerprint on the side of the crib.

CHAPTER NINETEEN

OPENING HIS EYES, DAVID Rush stared up at the ceiling and tried to work out why he'd just woken from a deep and peaceful sleep. He blinked, shocked by the realization that he was now wide awake, and then he turned and looked over at the other side of the bed.

To his immense relief, Mia was fast asleep.

Realizing that he was too awake, David climbed out of bed and headed over to the crib. Once he'd checked that Catherine was fine, he walked out onto the landing and made his way to the bathroom door, only to stop and look down the stairs as he realized that he'd just heard a faint bumping sound coming from one of the other rooms. Just as he began to remind himself that simple bumping sounds were nothing to worry about, he heard the same thing again, albeit a little more insistent this time.

"What the..."

He looked back at the bedroom door. He knew that both Mia and Catherine were asleep and that the house should be silent; there was no obvious storm raging outside, but a few seconds later he heard the same bumping sound yet again, and this time he realized that it seemed to be coming from the front room.

After hesitating as he tried to work out what he should do next, he began to make his way down the stairs, while silently cursing himself for not having any kind of weapon to hand.

Reaching the hallway, he looked through to the front room and waited, but now there was no hint of a disturbance. He told himself that he was being foolish, that he was in danger of becoming as paranoid as his wife, yet his heart was racing and he knew that those bumping sounds had to have been caused by something specific. Every ounce of his soul was screaming at him that he was making a mistake, that he was doing the one thing he'd always hated seeing in his wife, yet he couldn't help himself.

"You're being exactly like Mia!" a voice in the back of his head hissed.

Stepping into the front room, he reached out and switched the light on. He saw nothing untoward, nothing that made him in the least bit concerned, yet somehow that absence of trouble now became a problem; he'd heard a noise, he knew that something had to have been responsible, so now he felt sure that something was hiding nearby, playing a game or waiting for a chance to strike.

"If you say anything at all," the voice in the back of his head continued, "you're going to be a laughing stock. A hypocrite. You'll undo all the good work you ever did when you were helping fix Mia's mind."

He swallowed hard.

"Don't do this," the voice added. "Seriously, you'll never be able to live it down. Next time you have to tell Mia not to panic or overreact, you'll know that you don't have a leg to stand on. Is that what you want? Do you want to just collapse and become like her?"

He swallowed again, and this time his throat felt so very dry.

"Hello?" he said cautiously. "Is anyone there?"

He waited, and the only answer was a wall of silence that seemed almost to be mocking him. He stepped forward and immediately heard a creaking sound as the floorboard moved under his right foot; looking down he saw only carpet, but he thought of the floorboard hidden out of sight and he felt as if it had been waiting for him.

"Now's not the time for creepy noises," he whispered. "It's -"

Checking his watch, he saw that the time was almost three in the morning.

"It's 3am," he added with a sigh. "You should be asleep, not chasing shadows around the -"

Before he could finish, he heard another bump, this time coming from the far end of the room. He made his way over to that corner and saw only an armchair, yet he felt absolutely certain this time that something heavy had just knocked against a wall or the floor or the ceiling. He leaned over the chair and saw nothing behind, but a moment later he realized that the chair itself was slightly skew-whiff. Already there were marks on the carpet showing where this particular chair usually sat, yet he could see that the legs were occupying a different position. Reaching down, he moved the chair back into its proper spot, but he was already wondering why it had moved in the first place.

Crouching down, he peered under the chair as he tried to understand exactly what was happening. Finding nothing, he bent down further and leaned his head beneath the chair, still convinced that a magic answer was suddenly going to appear from out of somewhere.

"David?"

"What?"

He immediately tried to get up, only to bang

his head on the chair's hard underside. Feeling a crack of pain, he let out a gasp as he crawled back and looked over his shoulder, and then he let out a sigh as he saw his wife standing in the doorway with a quizzical expression on her face.

"What are you doing?" she asked.

"Nothing!" he replied, rubbing the top of his head.

"I woke up and you were gone," she continued. "You're not usually one for sneaking around in the middle of the night, David."

"I thought I heard something," he explained, still sitting on the floor.

"Like what?"

"I don't know. Like a bump... or a thud. I know how stupid it sounds. It sounds like something you'd have said a week or so ago."

"Thanks."

"You know I didn't mean it like that," he said, getting to his feet. "I just mean that I think your fears might have been contagious. I never used to worry about bumps in the night, and now look at me! I'm sneaking around in the wee small hours, chasing the tiniest little noises."

"I'm sure there's nothing to worry about," she told him. "Don't worry, I won't take it personally, but you should come back to bed."

"See?" he continued, unable to hide a sense of exasperation. "Do you see what's happening here?"

"I'm not sure what -"

"We've swapped!" he added. "You used to be the one getting freaked out by little imagined noises in the night, and I'd tell you not to worry. Now here I am, crawling around on all fours and looking under chairs at three o'clock at night, and you're telling me that everything's fine! When did we swap?"

"It's not a new house," she pointed out. "There are bound to be little... things in the night."

"Exactly! That's exactly the sort of thing I used to say to you!"

"You poor thing," she replied, stepping over to him and putting her hands on his shoulders. "You're not in a very good way right now, are you?"

"I'm just tired."

"And stressed," she added. "I can feel it in your shoulders, David. You're like a man who's got the weight of the world coming down on top of him. That's not good for you and inevitably cracks are going to show. I'm so sorry, I realize that some of this is my fault, I should have been more supportive instead of worrying about weird noises and things that were all in my head. You've obviously been through so much."

"Absolutely none of this is your fault," he told her.

"You can't stop me worrying," she replied,

before they both heard Catherine starting to cry again upstairs. "Hey, I should get back to her," she said, turning and heading out of the room, "but do you promise me you'll come up soon?"

"Of course."

"And you won't go chasing shadows again, will you? If you're not up in the next few minutes, I'm going to have to come back down and find you again."

"It won't come to that," he replied as he listened to her reaching the top of the stairs and going into the bedroom, followed by the sound of her talking to Catherine and trying to calm her down.

As the minutes passed and Catherine continued to cry, David realized that something else had changed. From the moment of her birth, Catherine had been a very happy baby who was by no means prone to massive crying fits; on the few occasions when she became upset, she'd always been quickly and easily pacified by Mia, who'd seemed to have a magic touch. As parents, David and Mia had joked so many times about her motherly instincts, and about the way she'd always been able to make Catherine feel better.

Now, as he walked to the door and looked at the stairs, David realized that Catherine's cries were actually getting louder. Mia was talking to her and trying to make the upset go away, but her efforts weren't working. If anything, Mia almost seemed to be making everything worse, and David couldn't help but wonder why this – along with so many other things – had suddenly flipped so completely.

CHAPTER TWENTY

SEVERAL WEEKS LATER, AS he slammed his car door shut and turned to make his way over to the office, David was surprised to see a familiar figure hurrying away from the building's front door.

"David!" Nick called out. "I've been looking everywhere for you!"

"What are you doing here?" David asked. "I thought -"

"I need to talk to you about your house," Nick continued, sounding a little breathless as he fumbled in his pockets and brought out his phone. "I tried to make Mia understand, but I think she's a little too scared, so I figured you might be a better bet. I couldn't go to the house, because she'd try to stop me, so I thought this was the best option."

"Have you been drinking?" David replied.

"Nick, don't take this the wrong way, but you look kind of awful. You look like you're five days into the kind of bender we used to go on when we were teens."

"I haven't slept too well lately," Nick said, struggling to unlock the phone with his trembling hands, "but that's just because I've been working on something. Did Mia mention the video footage that I had digitally enhanced?"

"Nick -"

"I'm not crazy!" Nick snapped suddenly, as if he'd been holding that assertion in for a long time. "Don't do it, David! You're my friend! Everyone else has been looking at me as if I've lost my mind, but I need you of all people to realize that I'm right!" He tried again to unlock his phone, but his fingers were shaking and he struggled to draw the correct pattern. "Just ignore the fact that I'm out of sorts right now," he continued. "Focus on the fact that something's really wrong in your house."

"Nick, I'm worried about you. It's not like you to be acting this way."

"I've got -"

Before he could finish, Nick dropped the phone, letting it fall to the ground. Hearing a cracking sound, he crouched down and picked the phone up, only to turn it over and find that the screen had shattered.

"Damn it!" he hissed, before throwing the

phone hard against the wall and then getting to his feet. "I still have the video in my photo gallery," he stammered, reaching toward David's pocket. "Give me your phone and I'll show you!"

"I'm not giving you my phone," David said firmly.

"I won't break it!" Nick replied. "Just give me your -"

"No!" David said, pushing him away. "Are you out of your mind? You look and sound like a complete lunatic! Do you realize that? You can't just turn up here at my office ranting and raving. How would Jackie feel if she could see you now?"

"Don't play that card!" Nick yelled, taking a step back and pointing at him. "Don't ever stoop to that level and try to emotionally blackmail me! I'd expect that from some people, David, but never from my best friend! I'm going to show you that video next time I see you, and I'm going to get more proof that something in your house killed Jackie! Then, when I've done all of that, everyone's going to have to see that I'm right! She didn't kill herself, David. Something in your house killed her, and I'm going to make you all see that!"

Picking up what remained of his phone, he turned and hurried away while muttering to himself under his breath.

"Hey, do you want to get a coffee?" David called after him, before letting out a heavy sigh.

"Great. I'm starting to think that I'm the only sane person round here right now."

***

"Who's Mummy's beautiful little girl?" Mia said, grinning from ear to ear as she lifted Catherine from her pram in the driveway and held her up for a moment. "You're so perfect. You realize that, don't you?"

Watching from behind some nearby bushes, Nick struggled to keep from yelling at her. He'd driven straight to the house after his confrontation with David, and he knew he had to somehow gather more evidence about whatever had happened to his wife. He watched as Mia set Catherine back into the pram and began to push her away, and then – once he was certain that the coast was clear – he crept around from behind the pram and made his way across the driveway.

Reaching the house, he slipped down the side and began to search for an open window. Unable to find anything, he hurried to the back door, only to find that this too was locked. He looked up, and finally he saw that the bathroom window had been left ajar, so he began to search for something he could use as a ladder. Stumbling across some old boxes, he piled them beneath the window and began to climb, struggling to remain steady until finally he managed to haul himself up to the open window.

After much huffing and puffing and maneuvering, he wriggled through the gap and dropped down into the bathroom.

"So much for living in the countryside," he muttered, brushing himself down. "You never know who might get inside if you leave your windows open."

He crept to the door and listened for a moment, but he knew everyone was out. Making his way onto the landing, he looked all around and tried to work out where he should try first; his original plan had been to film as much as possible, but he'd not managed to pick up a new phone yet so he figured that he simply needed to take a look around the house and hope that he could find some kind of evidence.

Stepping over to the master bedroom, he was about to go inside when he suddenly heard a muffled bumping sound coming from somewhere downstairs.

Heading across the landing, he looked down toward the hallway. The house had fallen silent, but a few seconds later he heard the bump again and this time he felt absolutely sure that someone or something was nearby. He hesitated, fully aware that he wasn't really prepared for what might happen next, and then he began to slowly creep down the stairs while listening out for any further hint as to who might be nearby.

Reaching the bottom of the stairs, he looked around again, before finally finding himself staring into the front room. Somehow, for reasons that he couldn't quite understand, he sensed that the bumping noise had come from this particular part of the house, so he stepped forward and looked around the room.

"Hello?" he said finally. "David? Mia?"

He waited, but in truth he was still sure they were both out.

"Anyone else?" he continued, as tears began to fill his eyes. "I'm not here to cause trouble, you know. I'd never do that. I'm here because I'm certain that Jackie didn't do all of those horrible things to herself, and because I just want to get to the truth. Can you understand that? I want to get to the truth so that I can understand what really happened to her, because until that happens I won't be able to move on."

He stepped over to the middle of the room, and now the first tears were starting to roll down his cheeks.

"I know there was someone else here that night," he added. "I don't know who you were, or what you wanted, but I saw you on that video. Please, can't you just tell me the truth?"

Turning, he looked all around the room, but

already he was starting to wonder whether he might have been mistaken, whether perhaps somehow that bumping sound had been caused by some random event like a bird hitting a window or some deep part of the building shifting slightly. What if, he realized now, he really was just some rambling drunken fool who couldn't get over his grief?

"Please," he continued desperately, "I only want -"

Before he could finish, he heard the bump again, this time very clearly coming from the corner of the room. He turned and looked in that direction, and he realized that the old armchair in the farthest corner was shaking slightly as the bumping sound continued.

"What the..."

Stepping forward, he tried to work out exactly what was happening. He grabbed the chair and moved it aside, and to his shock he saw now that the patch of carpet in the corner was shuddering, almost as if it was somehow being disturbed from beneath. Slowly he crouched down to take a closer look, and now the bumping sound was becoming more persistent. Reaching out, he found that the edge of the carpet was loose, so he began to slowly peel it back.

"Nick?"

Startled, he turned and saw that Mia was standing in the doorway, watching him with a concerned expression.

"I just popped back to fetch Catherine's bottle," she said cautiously, before taking a step forward and looking at the loose section of carpet. "What are you doing here? And what are you doing in that corner?" She hesitated, and after a few seconds her gaze narrowed. "You really shouldn't be in here, Nick."

CHAPTER TWENTY-ONE

"SO THEN NICK TURNED up," David said several hours later, standing in the kitchen with a glass of wine while Mia continued to cook the stir-fry, "and he looked diabolical. I'm really worried about him, but I'm not sure who to call."

"Hmm?" Mia replied, using a spatula to move some of the vegetables around the pan before turning to him. "Darling, I'm so sorry, I was miles away. What did you just say? Something about Nick?"

"He turned up at the office today."

"Why?"

"To rant about some conspiracy theory concerning Jackie's death."

"That's quite concerning," she replied, checking the noodles. "Do you think he's okay?"

"No," David said, before taking a sip of wine. "He's absolutely not okay."

"Obviously he's taking her death very hard," she said, heading to the sink and rinsing two glass bowls. "I know this probably isn't what you want to hear, but I actually don't think there's anything you can do to help." She turned to him. "I get it, he's your oldest friend and you want to fix his problems, but I'm worried you might just end up throwing more fuel onto the fire."

"What do you mean?"

"I mean that in his head, you – and me, and this house – are linked to Jackie's death. It might be better if we all just give him a wide berth for a little while and hope that he comes to his senses."

"So you don't think I should call him?"

"I think you're a great friend, but you need to take a step back." She paused for a moment. "I mean, you don't *actually* think for one second that anything nefarious happened to Jackie, do you?"

"Nefarious? No, of course not. It was obviously a suicide, no matter how hard that might be to accept." He took another sip of wine. "He's really going down some crazy rabbit-holes and coming up with the weirdest theories. It's almost as if he thinks that some kind of supernatural -"

"Dinner's ready," she said firmly, before he could get another word out. "Would you mind setting the table? And then can we please talk about anything except Jackie's horrible end? I'm sorry, I don't mean to sound heartless, but I think it's really disrespectful to her memory if we keep picking over the bones of what happened to her. She was in a terrible state and she hid it really well, right up until the end. Does it really have to be any more complicated than that?"

"No," he replied, although he seemed a little shocked by the bluntness of her comment. He stared at her for a moment longer, and then he took another sip of wine before taking some plates from the sideboard. "No, I suppose it doesn't."

***

"Wow!" he gasped, rolling back over onto his side of the bed as he tried to get his breath back. "That was just..."

His voice trailed off for a moment, before finally he turned to his wife.

"Wow!"

"I'm glad you approve," she replied with a faint smile, pulling the duvet cover up to hide her bare breasts.

"Can I ask you something?" he continued, rolling closer. "After Catherine was born you couldn't have been less interested in sex if you'd tried. Obviously I worked really hard to be a supportive husband, and I tried to avoid pressuring you while also making sure that you felt wanted. Most of the time, though, it felt as if nothing I did was ever going to work. I'd almost accepted that our days of regular love-making were over. So how come suddenly you're like this... sex maniac?"

"Are you complaining?" she asked.

"No!"

"Good," she replied, fixing him with a curious stare before allowing the faintest curl of a smile to reach her lips. "Because there's a lot more where that came from."

"I guess I'm just surprised by the change," he admitted, "but I'll get used to that. I might need to stock up on a few energy drinks, though, if you're going to be quite so physical."

Getting to his feet, he began to make his way over to the en suite bathroom.

"Can you tell any difference?" she asked suddenly.

He looked back at her.

"Between how it is now," she continued, "and how it was before? Sorry, I know this might seem like an odd question, but I was just wondering. Have you noticed anything different about our... intimate moments?"

"Apart from the fact that you're so into it now?"

"Apart from that," she replied. "I was just wondering whether you've noticed anything different in the way I am. In the way I touch you, or the way I kiss you, or... the way we make love. Or my body."

"That's getting a little deep, isn't it?"

"I don't know," she said. "*Is* it?"

"You seem a little more... carefree," he told her. "I don't know exactly what I mean by that. You seem more adventurous and open to different stuff. Sorry, I hope you're not offended."

"Of course I'm not. What exactly do you mean?"

"It's not like you were frigid before," he continued. "I'm comparing you to how it was before you got pregnant. I don't know, it's just like there was always this side of you that wasn't hugely adventurous or expressive in bed. You tended to kind of just take it. I don't mean you were a wet fish. Far from it. It's just that you tended to act a little subservient in the bedroom department, as if you thought your job was just to sort of... lean back and think of England. Sometimes I worried you weren't enjoying it quite as much as you should."

"And now?"

"Now you seem way more into what we're doing," he said, scratching the back of his neck. "Actually, the difference is like night and day. To be honest, it's a good job we don't have any neighbors nearby, otherwise there might have been some noise complaints. And that thing you do with your tongue is just... something else entirely."

"And which version of me do you prefer?"

"This version," he admitted. "There's not even any competition. Sorry, I hope that doesn't make me seem shallow, but I've always felt like a very sexual person, and the way you are now... I feel like, for the first time, I might actually struggle to keep up with you. But I like that. It's a challenge I really enjoy."

"I'm glad," she told him. "I only want to please you."

"I can't do anything more tonight," he said, turning and heading into the bathroom. "I hate to seem lazy, but do you mind checking on Catherine before we turn in? I honestly feel like I can barely even put one foot in front of the other."

"It's my pleasure," she said, climbing out of bed and slipping into her dressing gown, before making her way to the door. "I'm glad you agreed to try leaving her in her nursery for a night or two," she added. "I understand why we had her in the room with us, but I'm not sure it's good for her in the long-term. Or for us."

"I'll try anything once!" he called after her.

Once she was on the landing, Mia made her way past the top of the stairs. Stopping, she looked down toward the hallway and listened to the silence; she could hear the water running in the bathroom, but otherwise the house was entirely quiet, and she let out a sigh of relief as she wandered through to the nursery.

As she reached Catherine's crib, she looked down and saw that the child was asleep. For a moment she considered simply turning and leaving the room, but after a few seconds she couldn't resist reaching into the crib and picking Catherine up; peering into her face, she saw her eyes flickering open, and she felt a swelling sense of love in her chest.

"And what about you?" she whispered. "Do *you* feel any difference?"

She waited, but Catherine simply let out a faint gurgle.

"You shouldn't," Mia continued. "You realize that, don't you? I'm still your mother, so I don't want any silliness from you. Is that understood?"

This time Catherine began to cry.

"Don't do that," Mia said firmly, glaring at her. "What the hell's wrong with you? How many times do I have to prove to you that I'm still her? You know, you're actually starting to annoy me just a little."

Still crying, Catherine began to look around the room, as if she was searching for someone else.

"I'm right here!" Mia snarled, pulling her closer and staring directly into the child's eyes. "Don't look for other people. Don't pine for someone who's never coming back. *I'm* your mother, and I'm the only one you're ever going to need. So why don't you cut out this crying nonsense before I'm tempted to teach you a lesson you won't ever forget!"

She hesitated, before setting Catherine down again as if startled by her own anger.

"I'm sorry," she murmured, hurrying from the room. "Forgive me, I didn't mean to get angry like that."

***

Once she was back in the bedroom, Mia headed to the bed and then stopped. She could hear David in the bathroom, but a moment later he emerged and she turned to him. She opened her mouth to tell him what had just happened, before surprising herself by untying her robe and letting it fall to the floor, revealing her naked body.

"Nice view," he said, "but I'm *so* tired and -"

"Come and look at this," she replied, cutting him off with a hint of desperation in her voice. "Humor me."

He paused for a moment, before making his way over. Mia, meanwhile, cupped her own left breast so that he could see the nipple more clearly, revealing the tiniest hint of milk.

"Do you want to try it?" he asked with a

faint smile, sitting on the edge of the bed. "Straight from the source, I mean."

"Mia..."

"I know you've tried it from the bottle," she told him. "I saw you at the fridge one night. Did you like it?"

Clearly embarrassed, he started to blush as he glanced around the bedroom. When he turned to her again, he looked at the nipple as he felt his curiosity starting to mount. Finally, slowly, he knelt in front of her.

"Take some," she said softly, leaning forward until her breast was almost touching his lips. "I really want you to. I could see how much you liked trying it from the fridge. Now, David, I want you to drink it straight out of my body. What are you waiting for? There's nothing I wouldn't do for you, and I want to prove that. Nothing in this, or any other, world."

He looked up into her eyes for a few seconds, as if he still couldn't quite believe what he was hearing, and then he looked directly at her glistening nipple.

CHAPTER TWENTY-TWO

THUNDER RUMBLED IN THE distance as rain fell from a gray sky and blew down the outside of the windowpane.

"Nice day out there," David murmured, standing at the window with a cup of tea and watching the miserable scene. "Do you think we should get the barbecue out?"

"I'm going to take a shower!" Mia called through to him. "Can you listen out in case Catherine needs anything?"

"Will do," he replied, taking a sip of tea as he continued to watch the rain and listened to the sound of his wife heading upstairs. "You know," he continued, speaking to no-one in particular, "there's something strangely hypnotic about bad weather. Good weather's boring, but bad weather... I just can't stop watching the rain. Do you think there's something in that? Do you think it's some kind of poetic stirring?"

Fully aware that Mia could no longer hear him, he took a deep breath and tried to think of something profound to say about the awful weather. He supposed that he should try to paint the scene, although in truth he wasn't feeling very inspired; his father had always taunted him, telling him that he lacked the true soul of a real artist, and at times like this he found himself wondering whether the old man might have had a point. Shouldn't an artist leap to his easel, driven by a passionate desire to paint the power and fury of the natural world?

"You're no artist," he heard his father's voice sneering now. "This obsession with painting is just part of some childish adolescent bullshit you should have grown out of a long time ago. You've got a brilliant scientific mind! You should use it!"

David merely watched rain running own the other side of the glass and felt extremely glad that he wasn't out there. A moment later he saw a woman hurrying past, dressed head-to-toe in rainproof clothing, walking her dog; a faint smile crossed his lips as he thought of that poor woman caught in such bad weather, and again he was pleased not to be in the same situation.

Turning to head to the kitchen, he reached the middle of the room before suddenly hearing a sudden thump coming from somewhere below. He looked down at the carpet, and a moment later he realized that he could also hear a faint scratching sound. His first thought was that perhaps the house had attracted an infestation of mice or rats, but when he glanced at the far corner of the room he saw that the chair was once again slightly out of place, and that a section of the carpet was sticking up slightly.

Nonchalantly wandering over, he looked down and saw that this section of the carpet was slightly frayed. He crouched down and gave it a pull, and to his surprise he found that it came away fairly easily. He moved the chair aside, and then he pulled the carpet further back to reveal some kind of hatch set into the floorboards.

"What the hell is this?" he muttered, using the chair to prop the carpet up before grabbing a small metal ring on the hatch and lifting it up.

To his surprise, he found that the hatch opened to reveal a set of wooden steps leading down into the darkness beneath the house.

"Mia?" he called out. "Honey, I just found something that's going to blow your mind! Do you remember how we thought there wasn't a basement here?"

He peered into the darkness but saw only the top of the steps.

"We were wrong!" he continued. "Mia? Can

you believe this? We have a basement!"

He waited for a reply, before getting to his feet and heading out into the hallway. As he looked at the staircase, he realized he could hear the shower running upstairs.

"We have a basement," he said again, before turning to look back over at the corner. After a moment, he tilted his head. "What could be down there?"

***

Reaching the bottom of the rickety wooden steps, David switched on the flashlight and shone its beam across the low, small room. He saw thick cobwebs hanging down, but otherwise the space was empty, although after a moment he spotted a doorway leading through into another section.

"Mia's going to totally flip out when she sees this," he said to himself, with a growing sense of anticipation. "This is going to completely blow her mind."

Ducking down to avoid a low beam, he began to pick his way through the darkness, while also taking care to avoid touching any of the cobwebs. A few spiders recoiled from the light, trying to hide in the darkest corners, and as he made his way over to the opening David couldn't help but notice that the air was very damp and cold. He'd never had a huge amount of faith in the surveyor they'd used when they were buying the house, and now he was starting to realize that he should have trusted his instincts all along.

He ducked to step through the doorway, and then his left foot scuffed against something. Looking down, he let out a shocked gasp as he saw a leg on the floor; when he tilted the flashlight, he was horrified by the sight of a whole body resting on the concrete.

"What the hell?" he stammered, stepping around the body and shining the flashlight's beam down at its face, only to realize that he recognized its features. "Nick?"

Crouching down, he nudged the body's shoulder, but he could already see that he was too late. Nick's dead, glassy eyes were staring over at the far wall, but for a few seconds David was unable to comprehend exactly what he'd found. He told himself that there had to be a mistake, and then he noticed a thick, glistening and very bloody wound on the back of his friend's head, as if he'd been hit repeatedly by something heavy and blunt.

Getting to his feet, and trying not to panic, David turned to hurry back upstairs. As he stepped over Nick's body, however, he froze as he realized that he could hear a faint whimpering sound coming from nearby.

"Who's there?" he called out, turning and

shining the flashlight across the empty space. "Who -"

Before he could finish, he realized that something was moving in the far corner. He felt a shudder pass through his chest as he slowly raised the flashlight, and then he froze again as he saw a pair of trembling, tightly-bound feet covered in bloodied scratches. Raising the flashlight further, he found himself staring in horror at a naked woman tied and bound in the corner, shaking violently with her head bowed and her hair covering her features.

"What the hell?" he said again, keeping the flashlight's beam fixed on the woman as he began to step toward her. "Who are you? What -"

Suddenly the women let out a terrified shriek and turned away, as if she was trying to curl herself into such a tiny ball that no-one would be able to see her at all.

"Hey, I'm not going to hurt you!" David stammered, still trying to work out exactly he'd discovered beneath his house. "My name's David Rush, and this is my basement and -"

The woman turned to him, and as tangled hair fell down across her face he was just about able to make out a terrified eye staring back at him. She was trying to speak, but a thick patch of fabric had been taped over her mouth, keeping her from managing anything more than a faint mumbled moan.

"Hang on," David said, stepping closer as he realized that he recognized the woman from somewhere. "I'm going to take that thing off your mouth, okay?"

She pulled back slightly, as if she was still terrified, but he carefully knelt in front of her and held up one hand in an attempt to show that he was friendly.

"How long have you been down here?" he asked, before reaching out and moving the hair from across her face. "Why are -"

In that moment, he understood how he recognized her. He stared in wild, blinking shock, convinced that he had to be wrong; the more he stared, however, the more he realized that he was right. She was bloodied and bruised, with a swollen cut on her cheek, and her eyes were reddened and fearful; she'd clearly lost weight, and her unkempt hair made her look almost completely different, but as he tilted his head slightly David knew that there had been no mistake. Even though the entire situation had to be impossible, as he stared at the trembling naked woman he knew that he had to say her name.

"Mia?"

Recognizing his wife, he reached out and began to peel the patch from across her mouth.

"Mia, I don't understand," he stammered, "how did you get down here so fast? You were just in the shower and -"

"Run!" she screamed, so loudly that he could almost hear the back of her throat shredding. "Get out of here! Save Catherine! David, you have to run!"

CHAPTER TWENTY-THREE

"MIA, WHAT ARE YOU doing down here?" David asked. "Who -"

"Run!" she yelled again, before looking past him as if she'd spotted something. "It's too late! Kill her! David, you have to kill her!"

Startled, he turned to see a figure standing in the doorway, a little way past Nick's crumpled body. Raising his flashlight, he saw to his astonishment that this woman was also Mia, wearing nothing but a towel following her shower. He stared at her face, then he turned to the naked woman in the corner, and then he turned to the woman in the doorway. In that moment he felt as if reality itself had begun to break down, as if somehow the entire universe had come to a screeching and inexplicable halt.

Somehow, impossibly, the two women were

both Mia Rush.

"David," the Mia in the doorway said calmly, holding up her hands, "I want you to listen to me very carefully. This will all make -"

"Get away from him!" the other Mia screamed. "Leave my family alone!"

"I don't know what's going on here," David said, getting to his feet as he continued to look between the two women. "Which of you is my wife?"

"I am," the Mia in the doorway said.

"No, it's me!" the Mia in the corner shouted furiously. "David, I'm me! I'm right here!"

"It's complicated," the woman in the doorway continued, before letting out a heavy sigh. "I knew I was going to have to explain things eventually, but I thought I'd have more time. I suppose I should have just bitten the bullet, though. It was always going to come out a little wrong if I had to do it under pressure."

She stepped forward.

"I'm -"

"David, don't let her near you!" the Mia on the floor shouted. "She attacked me and tied me up down here! She killed Nick!"

"I need to explain," the other woman replied.

"I bet she killed Jackie too!" the other Mia hissed. "Admit it! You killed her!"

"Yes," the Mia in front of the doorway said, as if that answer was completely normal. "I have no problem confirming the truth. I killed Jackie and Nick, and if I'm being completely honest, I would have killed you too." She stared down at the other Mia for a moment. "Fortunately for you," she added, "a small complication got in the way of that part of the plan."

"Wait a moment," David said, feeling as if his head was about to explode, "can someone please explain to me what's going on?"

"Why did I leave it so long?" the Mia in the towel asked, clearly frustrated. "I knew something like this was going to happen if I waited, but I just couldn't bring myself to take the risk." She paused, before sitting on the edge of an old packing case. "I can explain everything, David, but I need you to listen and really hear what I'm saying to you. Some of this might sound... improbable."

"I'm listening," he told her.

"No!" the Mia in the corner yelled, grabbing his leg and trying to pull him closer as tears streamed down her face. "David, you have to get help! This woman, this *thing*, is a murderer!"

David opened his mouth to reply, before falling still once more as he looked from one woman to the other.

"Is one of you a clone?" he asked finally. "Is that what's happening here?"

"You have no idea how lucky you two are," the Mia on the box continued. "Where I come from, my David and I tried so many times for a baby. The doctors told us we had a one in a million chance of conceiving, less even, but we refused to take no for an answer. I actually, genuinely lost count of how many IVF rounds we went through, constantly trying over and over again to conceive. We knew the odds were against us, but somehow I think we both thought that we'd beat those odds, that we'd be the ones to get a miracle."

"*Your* David?" David said cautiously. "What do you mean by that?"

"Where I come from," she explained, "my David stuck to his original plan and became a scientist. A theoretical physicist, actually. He wanted to work in the art world, but his father pretty much forced him to continue with the more respectable pathway, and eventually he became one of the most brilliant minds of his generation. He was rich and successful, and respected around the world, and as his wife I got to benefit from his success. We had everything money could possibly buy, our lives were perfect, but all we were missing... was a child."

"Who are you?" David whispered.

"We could have adopted," she admitted. "Everyone said we should, but we wanted a child of our own. Meanwhile, David's work had begun to develop, and he'd made some discoveries that seemed truly impossible. Over time, as he experimented, he realized that we could look beyond our own world. Beyond our own universe. Did you know that there are millions, perhaps trillions, of different universes out there? There's a multitude of worlds, some of them only different to one another by the tiniest little factors. That's what we discovered when we started searching, using some advanced tracking technology to search for a certain biological marker. You know how they find new planets these days by detecting hints of their presence? They don't actually see them, but they pick up signs that they exist. Well, that's what we did. We searched universe after universe for the biological marker of a child born to some variant of Mia and David Rush."

"This is insane," David said, shaking his head slowly.

"The search was slow at first," she told him, "until we used artificial intelligence to vastly speed it up. And out of hundreds of millions of universes that we searched, do you know how many of them were universes in which Mia and David Rush managed to have a healthy child?"

She paused, before holding up a single finger.

"One," she added, with a hint of amazement in her voice. "This one."

"You're not Mia," David replied, as the other woman continued to cling to his leg. "You can't be."

"So naturally the next step was to find a way to come here," the woman on the box continued. "I want to be quite clear that our original plan was very different. David was convinced that there had to be a reason why the versions of us in this universe had been successful when all the others had failed. He thought that we could study you and find out what you'd done differently, why your IVF treatment had succeeded where all the others had gone wrong. He told me that we could do all of that without you guys ever noticing that we existed."

"I'm dreaming," David stammered. "I have to be. That's the only explanation."

"But it was taking too long," she explained. "You've got to admit, I've never been a very patient woman. I'm pretty sure that's one of my innate qualities, it's probably true in every universe."

"You're a liar!" the other Mia shouted. "You're not me! You can't be me!"

"All I ever wanted was to be a mother," the Mia on the box said sadly. "Do you have any idea how much that drove me? I always said that I'd do *anything* to make my dream come true, and I really meant that. I didn't want anyone to get hurt but, well, sometimes that's impossible to avoid. To be honest, I didn't know just how far I was willing to go. Not until I was already well past the point of no return."

"David, get me out of here," the Mia on the floor whimpered, pulling on his leg. "I've been down here for days now! She hasn't fed me or even given me any water!"

"I'm sorry about that," the other Mia said, "but when I got here, I found to my surprise that I couldn't kill you. Not directly, at least. I wanted to, I tried to, but something held be back. I could kill other people in this universe, but for some reason that my David would probably have been able to understand, I seem to be unable to kill another version of myself. Neglecting you, on the other hand, seems to have been working fairly well so far, so perhaps that's a useful little loophole. Honestly, if I'd just been able to keep this place a secret for a little while longer, I'm confident you would have died anyway."

"Bitch!" the Mia on the floor screamed. "You won't get away with this!"

"I came from an entirely different universe," the Mia on the box continued, "because this is the only world in which I'm able to be a mother. Out of all the millions of parallel universes, out of the entire multitude of different realities, *this* is the one where Catherine was conceived. That really makes her a miracle child, don't you think? And the thing is, having come this far, there's absolutely no way I'm going to let anyone stop me. After all, the David from my world tried to do that, right at the end. And that really didn't end too well for him."

CHAPTER TWENTY-FOUR

Several weeks earlier...

THE LIGHTS OF THE city twinkled beyond the penthouse's windows. Still wearing the dress she'd worn to the charity gala, Mia Rush stared out at London and tried to ignore the sad ache in her heart.

A moment later, hearing footsteps, she turned to see her husband David returning from the bathroom.

"Tired?" she said with a faint smile.

"Exhausted," he admitted. "I'm sorry, I know you didn't want to go tonight, but I needed to hobnob with those bigwig assholes who make the funding decisions. That's the side of life as a scientist that nobody ever wants you about. The politics are -"

"Let's do it tonight," she said suddenly, interrupting him.

"Do what?"

"You know damn well what," she continued, fixing him with a determined stare. "We've been talking about it for so long, we've pussy-footed around the possibilities for long enough, and now the time has come to take some action. I understand why you haven't told anyone else about the technology you developed, I understand that it can be dangerous, but I can't wait any longer."

"It's not that easy," he said with a sigh. "I still need to figure out a way to scan the other versions of us in more detail and analyze their -"

"I'm not talking about scanning anyone," she said, still holding her half-empty glass of wine as she stepped toward him. "I'm sick and tired of that nonsense. I'm talking about taking what's rightfully ours."

"I'm not sure I completely follow," he told her cautiously, although the fear in his eyes suggested that he had a good idea.

"Our child," she continued, with tears in her eyes. "I'm talking about our child, David. Sure, she might have been conceived by versions of us in an alternative world, but that doesn't make her any less our child. And from what we've seen of the others, they're not equipped to raise her the way that we'd raise her. We have money, David. She'll want for nothing."

"What exactly are you suggesting?"

"You know exactly what I'm suggesting," she replied. "Let's not waste time trying to study the other me and the other you. Let's just take that beautiful child and bring her here to our world, where she could be loved and looked after and given every possible opportunity in life."

"Are you talking about stealing a baby?"

"I'm talking about taking *our* baby!" she snapped angrily, before taking a moment to compose herself. "There's a difference, and you know it. We're the best possible versions of ourselves, so doesn't it stand to reason that we should be the ones who raise little Catherine? If we take her now, she'll never have any idea that she was born in that other universe. And if you think about it in the right way, we wouldn't even be doing anything wrong."

"Mia -"

"You can't steal from yourself," she added. "We'd simply be reallocating her to our world, so that she gets the best of everything. Come on, David, you know I'm right. The time has come to be brave, and to take action. So why don't we go and get her tonight?"

He opened his mouth to reply, before hesitating as she stepped closer and put her hands on his shoulders.

"She's ours anyway," she purred, looking deep into his eyes. "We've always wanted to be parents, David, and now our chance is here. So let's be the best parents any child could ever have!"

***

Several hours later, Mia stood in the penthouse's dining room and watched as David tapped at his laptop. She'd been pacing back and forth for a while now, impatiently waiting for him to declare that everything was ready, and now she felt as if she might be about to scream.

"Well?" she said finally.

"One moment."

"You keep saying that," she reminded him. "How many more moments will it take before we can do this? It's like the first time you made your own marmalade. Why do you always have to fuss instead of just diving in?"

She took another sip of wine, and then she looked at the laptop's screen and saw all sorts of charts and figures; very little about the machine made sense to her, although over the years she'd picked up the basics.

"And you're sure this will allow us to actually travel there?" she continued, feeling a little breathless now as her sense of anticipation became stronger. "Then we can bring her back?"

"One moment."

"Please don't say that again," she said through gritted teeth. "It's driving me round the -"

Before she could finish, she saw the telltale symbols on the screen that meant the machine was shutting down. She looked at the gate ahead; two vertical poles marked the edges of the space where the portal was supposed to appear, but those poles too were shifting back into an idle status.

"What are you doing?" she asked.

"I'm being the sane one," David said, getting to his feet and turning to her. "I thought I could allow us to go and steal that child, but now I've come to my senses. Mia, I know you hate it when people say this to you, but we *can* still adopt and -"

"No!" she said firmly.

"We can't go and steal someone else's child," he continued, making his way over to her. "It's wrong."

"It's not wrong," she replied, "because it's technically already our child!"

"No," he said, shaking his head, "it'll be coming from a whole different universe, from a world where it has loving parents who care for it very much. Can't we just be happy that this Catherine child exists? Sure, she might be a whole world away, but she's out there and she's real and she's proof that we could have had a child of our own if... well, if we'd been the lucky ones."

"Are you seriously suggesting," she replied darkly, "that you want us to give up?"

"We can adopt and -"

"If you say that one more time," she murmured, tightening her grip on the wineglass, "I won't be responsible for my actions."

"I promise you that it'll all be okay," he continued. "You know you can trust me, Mia, don't you? Everything will be fine, we'll adopt a child of our own and -"

"Never!" she screamed, lunging at him in a fit of fury and slamming her fist against the side of his head. She heard the wineglass break, but she paid no attention as she hit him again, and then as he slumped to the floor she dropped down onto his chest and hit him repeatedly. "Stop saying that!" she shouted. "You're supposed to be on my side! We talked about this, David! We're supposed to be a team! We're supposed to be -"

Stopping suddenly, she saw to her horror that the wineglass had broken and that the jagged stem was digging into his jugular. She instinctively pulled the wineglass away, and blood immediately started bursting from the wound. As David let out a series of agonized gasps and tried to get up, Mia could only pull back and watch in shocked silence as he slumped back down while still clutching his wounded neck. More and more blood was flowing down onto the floor and spraying against the wall, and finally David leaned over onto his side and let out one final pained groan.

Staring at him, Mia waited for him to say something.

"David?" she stammered finally, as tears filled her eyes. After a moment she crawled over and rolled him onto his back, only to see his lifeless eyes staring toward the ceiling. "David, no, come back!" she gasped, shaking him violently. "David, you can't leave me alone!"

She shook him for a few more seconds before stopping, and in her heart of hearts she already knew that he was gone.

"I didn't mean to do it!" she whimpered. "I was just angry, that's all! It's your fault for saying you were going to stop us! It's your fault for..."

Her voice trailed off, and after a moment she turned and looked over at the laptop, then at the metal poles a little further off. Her mind was racing, but she realized after a few seconds that she certainly knew how to switch the entire machine on, in which case...

"I won't be alone," she said softly, as a sense of hope began to fill her heart once more. "I'll show you, David. I'll show you that you were wrong. I'm going to find Catherine and bring her back, and I'm going to make our family whole again!"

Getting to her feet, she walked over to the laptop and tapped at the keys. Within a couple of minutes she'd managed to get the lead generator started, and she knew now that she just had to wait a few more seconds for the portal to open.

"I'm coming, Catherine," she said, as the portal burst into life, its light filling her eyes. "Mummy's coming to get you!"

CHAPTER TWENTY-FIVE

LETTING OUT A SHOCKED gasp, she fell forward and landed with a bump on the floor. For a moment, feeling as if every atom in her body had been ripped apart and rearranged, she was barely able to remember her own name, but over the next few seconds her mind began to pull back together.

Looking around, she found that she was on the landing of what seemed to be a nice little rural house. She'd seen images of the house before, shown to her by David when he'd been searching the various alternate universes, and now she'd finally arrived; getting to her feet, she began to take in her surroundings, although a moment later she saw a few flames flickering across one of the nearby walls.

Stepping closer to the wall, she realized that this was where the portal had appeared. She reached out and touched the surface; already the flames were dying out, leaving a blackened smudge that had caused the wallpaper to blister in places. Taking a deep breath, she realized in that moment that after so much planning, she'd finally made the jump. She'd never doubted her husband, of course, yet she still couldn't quite believe that all the planning had come to fruition.

Touching the blistered wallpaper, feeling a gentle warmth, she thought of her home. She had no way of ever getting back there, and she felt tears in her eyes as she thought of David's corpse on the floor in their apartment.

"I'm so sorry," she whispered, as the first tear ran down her cheek. "David, I really didn't mean to hurt you or -"

Before she could finish, she heard the sound of footsteps downstairs. Pulling back, she tried not to panic as she realized that somebody else was in the house, and she began to look around for somewhere she might be able to hide.

"Hello?" she heard her own voice calling out from the hallway. "Is someone there?"

***

"That's totally not what happened," Jackie was saying, her voice sounding so clear as it drifted through from the dining room. "David fell out of the tree *after* everyone had seen him through the window."

"Okay," David replied, "I think I should clarify a few details of this story before I end up sounding like a complete tool."

"We're way past that moment," Nick interjected.

Having held back for so long, the other Mia had now been drawn out into the hallway, desperate to eavesdrop on the conversation.

"This is my favorite story from our college days," Jackie continued. "Mia, honestly, if you'd known David back then you'd have seen a very different side to him."

"I can't believe there was a time when he struggled to talk to girls," the original Mia replied. "The David I met a few years ago was so suave and sophisticated. I mean, when we first got talking in that bar and he told me all about how he'd switched from science to art in his career, I was swept up in the whole thing. I thought he was this amazing guy who could probably pick up any girl he wanted in the whole world. Honestly, I just couldn't believe that he was interested in me at all."

"So he was hiding in a tree perving on this girl," Jackie replied, "and -"

"That is totally not what was happening," David protested. "I'd actually climbed up there because I wanted to take a photo of a nearby cemetery, and I had no idea that those girls from our English class lived in the house next door."

Still listening from the hallway, the other Mia struggled to hold back tears. She'd heard the same story from her David, back in her world, and she was shocked that so many incidents had occurred in both places. Part of her desperately wanted to join in and take part in the dinner party, but of course she knew she couldn't possibly do that. Not yet, at least.

Not until she'd completed her plan.

***

Examining the breast pump, the other Mia turned it around and began to wonder whether it could be modified in some way. She would never normally have considered such a horrific plan, but she was coming to truly hate the other version of herself, despising her for seemingly taking such happiness for granted.

"Little metal teeth," she whispered, and in the back of her mind she could already hear bones cracking. "That would work if the suction was massively enhanced and -"

"Hey," Jackie said, suddenly stepping into the kitchen, "what are you doing up so late?"

Startled, the other Mia turned and watched as Jackie headed over to the sink and poured herself a glass of water. This version of Jackie was similar to the one she knew, but a little plumper and with no dye in her hair.

"I think I'm aging prematurely," Jackie continued nonchalantly. "I swear, I can't go through the whole night without getting up to pee, and then I always need a glass of water. Of course, it's probably different for you, what with the baby. That's one of the many reasons I've never wanted kids of my own. I think, deep down, I'm too selfish."

After drinking the glass of water, she turned and furrowed her brow.

"Are you okay over there, Mia?" she asked cautiously. "You look... bothered."

"Me?" the other Mia replied.

"What's wrong?" Jackie continued, making her way over. "You know, I thought you seemed a little off during dinner. I told myself it was probably 'cause of the baby, but I also figure that might be a little mean of me. Just because you're a mother now, that doesn't mean you can't have other feelings as well." She stopped in front of her, grinning as she waited for a response. "You know you can tell me anything, right?" she added. "Just because I knew David long before I knew you, I hope you don't feel like there's some kind of divide between us. I've always wanted us to be friends."

"Indeed."

"I'm probably just bugging you," Jackie added, patting her hard on the side of the arm before looking at the breast pump in her hands. "Oh, wait, did I interrupt you when you were about to..." She sighed. "It's booby time, right? I've got to say, I really don't get how that works." Reaching over, she grabbed the pump and began to examine it carefully. "I don't really like the idea of having my boob pumped, if that makes sense. I suppose it's different for you when you've got milk in there. Does it hurt if you don't get it out? Does it get swollen?"

"I -"

"Have you tasted it?" she continued excitedly. "Has David? Wow, I only just realized how tempting that must be!" She set the pump down loudly on the table, before turning to go to the fridge. "Man, I don't want to sound like some kind of pervert, but I'd actually like to try some myself. Do you think you could make ice cream with it? I know that makes me sound like I'm totally sick in the head, but actually -"

Before she could stop herself, the other Mia grabbed the pump and smashed it against the side of Jackie's head. Shocked, Jackie pulled back and slipped, falling against the side of the counter and smacking her head on the edge. After letting out a shocked gasp, she fell to the floor, and now her dead eyes stared out across the floor.

"Jackie?" the other Mia said cautiously. "Are you okay?"

She waited for an answer, and then she began to look around. She knew she couldn't afford to draw attention to herself, and that she needed to find a way to make Jackie's death look less suspicious. She hesitated for a few seconds, before crouching down and checking the dead woman's pockets. Almost immediately, she found a set of car keys; looking over at the darkened window, she was already coming up with a plan.

***

Staring out the window, she watched as the original

Mia pushed the pram along the driveway. A moment later, hearing the sound of water running, she turned and looked toward the bathroom.

After a moment, sure that she wouldn't be spotted right now, she crept to the door and looked inside. She saw David standing naked in the shower with his back to her, and she felt an immediate fluttering sense of longing in her chest. She'd been struggling to accept what she'd done to her own David, she'd been overcome by a sense of guilt, but now she began to wonder whether she might be able to make amends. As she watched him showering, she realized that she'd perhaps been a little too cautious, and that the time had come to make her move.

"It's all going to be alright soon," she purred softly under her breath. "We're going to be the happy little family we always should have been."

A moment later, feeling a hint of wetness in her bra, she looked down. She moved the top of her shirt aside and saw to her shock that her breasts seemed slightly larger, as if her body had begun to react to the presence of a child. No, to the presence of *her* child.

"It's all coming together," she whispered. "This is a sign from above that I'm doing the right thing."

CHAPTER TWENTY-SIX

Today...

"I MADE MISTAKES," THE same Mia said now, still sitting on the packing box wrapped in a towel, with wet hair hanging down to her shoulders. "I didn't realize that once I arrived, I'd be stranded. I have no idea how to get back. So I had to come up with a better plan. I couldn't just snatch Catherine and leave."

"I *have* to be dreaming," David said again.

"So I don't really have a choice," the other Mia continued, getting to her feet. "If I'm stuck here, then I have no choice but to take over all duties relating to Catherine. She's my daughter as much as she's yours and -"

"Liar!" the Mia on the floor screamed.

"You're nothing! Do you hear me? You're not her mother!"

"Now you're just trying to upset me," the other Mia replied. "My body has even begun to react to her presence. I don't know exactly how hormones work, but I've even been able to feed her myself."

"Tell her, David!" the first Mia shouted, turning to her husband. "Tell her that this is madness! Tell her that she can't just come here and do all of this!"

"I always had an interest in parallel universes," he replied, with a faraway gaze in his eyes. "Before I insisted on entering the art world, when Dad was still trying to get me to pursue a career in science, parallel universes were the one area of study that I thought I might be able to stomach. Eventually I was strong enough to insist on art, but I've often wondered..."

His voice trailed off.

"You were brilliant," the other Mia said, with tears in her eyes. "Truly brilliant. I wouldn't be here now if you hadn't come up with all your wonderful ideas and turned them into reality. Seeing you work, and listening to you explaining all your wonderful theories, was such a wonderful honor. You have no idea how much I always admired your intelligence, David." Hearing Catherine crying upstairs, she got to her feet and headed to the open doorway. "I should go to her."

"Don't touch her!" the first Mia snarled, trying to get to her feet, only for the straps to keep her on the floor. "You're not allowed near her!" she yelled as the other Mia disappeared from view and headed up into the house. "Do you hear me? Leave her alone!"

"Brilliant?" David whispered. "Did you hear that? I could have been brilliant."

"Untie me!" she hissed, struggling again to get free. "David, we have to stop her! She's going to take Catherine!"

"Of course," he replied, kneeling next to her and trying to pull the straps away, only to find that they were held too firmly in place. "Hold on a moment, I can't quite work out how -"

"There's no time!" she shouted, pushing him away. "Hurry, David! You have to stop her before she takes Catherine away forever!"

***

"It's okay," the other Mia said, standing in the bedroom and gently lifting Catherine from her crib, "there's no need to cry. Mummy's here now."

She began to gently rock the child, who slowly stopped crying.

"There," this Mia continued, "isn't that all better? You recognize Mummy, don't you? Of course you do. It's all about pheromones and instinct, and those are two things that aren't restricted to just one universe. I'm your mother, just as much as she is. She might have given birth to you, but that really doesn't mean very much."

Leaning down, she kissed Catherine on the forehead.

"I love you, my beautiful little darling."

"How long have you been here?" David asked, stopping in the doorway. "When did you make the switch?"

"When I arrived, I was dazed," she replied, as she continued to rock Catherine. "I literally fell through a hole in one of the walls. When the hole sealed up, there were a few marks, but I managed to hide. After that I lurked for a while so that I could regain my strength, although I couldn't help observing the three of you. I'd done my research before I came, and I knew there was a basement in this house that you'd apparently missed, so that gave me some breathing space."

"Did you kill Jackie?"

"She surprised me," she explained. "I panicked, and she would have blown my cover. I did what I had to do."

"And then you swapped places with the real Mia."

"*I'm* the real Mia," she replied, turning to him. "Or we both are. You know what I mean. She was getting in the way, and I saw my chance one time while you were out. I meant to kill her so that she wouldn't suffer, but I found that I just couldn't. It's hard to describe, but whenever I made an attempt to end her life, I felt as if I just couldn't go through with it. Perhaps one day I'll understand how that works. I decided to tie her up and put her in the basement instead where you wouldn't find her, but then Nick showed up and apparently he'd caught me on camera during your party night, so I had to get him out of the way as well. You know what they say about the best laid plans, don't you?"

"I want you to put Catherine down."

"I can't do that."

"She's not your child."

"Oh, but she is," she purred, smiling as Catherine giggled at her. "She's my beautiful little angel, and I love her more and more with each passing day. She's everything I ever dreamed of."

"Put her down and -"

"She has your eyes, you know," she added, glancing at him. "Has the other Mia ever told you that? Catherine has your eyes. Your intelligence."

David hesitated, before stepping over to take a look.

"Do you see?" she asked.

"Maybe," he admitted. "So did I really invent this whole mechanism for traveling here? Did I come up with some kind of way to... peel away the barriers between one universe and the next?"

"Impressed?"

"Kind of," he told her. "I always thought I could do well in science, but I followed my instinct for the arts. The funny thing is, it was Mia... my Mia... who really encouraged me to do that. I'd already rebelled, but I probably would have drifted back eventually. If it hadn't been for her, I might very well have stuck to the things my father wanted me to study. Mia taught me the value of rebelling."

"Do you want to know something curious?" she replied. "We observed so many different universes, and you were a scientist in all of them. This universe was the only one where you and your Mia had a child, and also the only one where you went against the sciences. I can't help but wonder whether there's a correlation there."

"Was I rich in that other universe?"

"A millionaire many times over."

"And famous?"

"Fairly, and you would have become the most famous man in history if your discoveries had been made public. You'd have won the Nobel prize, and that would have just been for starters. You'd have been more famous than Einstein."

"Instead here I am, getting all excited about gallery openings."

"Is that so bad?" she asked. "You have

Catherine."

"And you killed that version of me, right?" he added, turning to her with a hint of concern in his eyes. "Does that really mean there's no way for you to go back home?"

"Looks like I'm stuck here," she admitted, before pausing for a moment. "I didn't mean to kill him. It's just that he had a kind of last-minute moral panic, and in turn I lost control briefly. I hope you realize that in ordinary circumstances I would never, ever have done anything to hurt you." She paused again. "I love you far too much."

"It's weird hearing you say that," he replied. "It's almost as if..."

"I kept thinking that you'd be able to tell the difference," she continued. "Between me and her, I mean. Especially when we made love, I was so sure that you'd realize something was wrong. You didn't, though, did you? And I suppose that means that nothing was wrong at all, not really. Isn't that rather significant?"

"I feel awful," he told her. "I *should* have felt the difference."

"But you didn't," she said softly, "and there's absolutely no need for you to ever feel bad about anything. You're a wonderful man, David. You're just like the David I left behind in my own world." She paused, watching him carefully, and slowly a smile began to spread across her lips. "I understand why you're finding this so difficult," she continued, "and I'd never want to do or say anything to minimize your struggle, but... are you sure you've really thought this all through? What if there was another option open to you? What if you didn't have to go back to the way things were?"

CHAPTER TWENTY-SEVEN

PULLING AS HARD AS she could manage on the leather restraints, Mia – the original Mia – refused to let the blood stop her. The restraints had begun to wear through the flesh around her wrists, but she knew she had to keep going and hurry upstairs to help David.

"Come on!" she hissed, frantically trying to find some way to get free. "What -"

Hearing footsteps, she turned and looked across the basement. She braced herself, terrified that the other Mia might have somehow gained the upper hand again, but a moment later David stepped into view.

"Thank you!" she gasped, letting out a heavy sigh of relief. "Did you stop her? David, where is she? Did you kill her?"

"Honey -"

"I was so worried," she continued, finally leaning back against the wall as she felt a rush of relief flooding through her body. Tears streamed down her face as she allowed herself to believe that the nightmare was over. "Can you find some way to get me out of here? Hey, wait, is Catherine okay? Did you check on her first?"

He made his way over to her.

"She's okay, right?" she continued, watching his face as she began to sense that something wasn't quite right. "David, tell me that she's okay!"

She waited for a response, and now all sorts of terrible thoughts were rushing through her mind.

"David!" she shouted. "Tell me that Catherine's okay!"

"Catherine's okay," he replied nervously.

"Are you sure?"

He nodded.

"She must be traumatized," she continued. "She's young, though, so hopefully it won't be anything that lasts too long. We'll consult a therapist and see what they suggest, but I'm sure she'll bounce back soon." She pulled on the restraints again. "Can you *please* find a way to get me out of these?" she added. "I have to go to her! I have to make her see that I'm her real mother!"

Again she waited, but David was simply standing over her with a strangely calm expression on his face.

"David?" she said, trying not to panic too much. "What -"

Before she could finish, she heard more footsteps. Turning, she saw to her horror that the other Mia was making her way through into the room.

"David, it's her!" she shouted. "Did you knock her out? She's awake again! David, look out!"

"Did you tell her?" the other Mia asked.

"Tell me what?" the first Mia stammered, looking up at her husband. "David, what's this crazy bitch talking about?"

"You know it has to be you," the other Mia said, and she too was staring at David. "I'd do it if I could, but something keeps stopping me. It has to be you, but it only needs to take a few minutes and then it'll all be over. I could maybe find another loophole, but I'd rather have it done cleanly, plus I want you to prove that you understand. The best approach is just to rip the band-aid off and get it done. I can help with the clean-up, and with all the other logistics. I just can't perform the actual act itself."

"David, what's going on?" the first Mia asked, before reaching out and grabbing her husband's hand. "David, why aren't you doing anything?"

"This isn't fair on her," the other Mia continued. "David, seriously, we talked about this. You mustn't drag it out."

"I know," he murmured.

"Then get it done," the other Mia said, before turning to her double on the floor. "Come on, the David from my universe would at least have the balls to do the right thing." She waited, and then she sighed as she made her way over and nudged him out of the way. "Fine," she muttered, staring down at the first Mia, "I know this is going to be hard for you, but it's the best thing for all concerned. Well, not for you, but for everyone else."

"What are you talking about?" the first Mia asked, staring at her for a moment longer before looking up at David again. "Can someone please tell me what the hell's going on?"

"It'll all be over soon," the other Mia told her. "Believe me, I take no comfort in any of this. Just, please, remember that we all want the same thing. We all want Catherine to have a happy life."

"What does she mean?" the first Mia stammered, increasingly disturbed by David's demeanor and by his strange reluctance to help her. "David? You're really starting to scare me now, David. What's happening?"

***

Stepping out through the back door, Mia stumbled slightly as she tried to process everything that David had told her. Convinced that she must have misunderstood, or that she must be dreaming, she stopped and tried to turn to him; in that moment he pushed her hard in the back, forcing her to keep going.

"You can't be serious," Mia said, stopping again. "I'm not -"

Before she could finish, she felt the knife's tip once again pressing against the small of her back. She flinched, telling herself that David would never actually hurt her, but a moment later she felt a hand touching her shoulder from behind.

"I'm going to let the two of you have some privacy," the other Mia said. "David, I can trust you to go through with this, can't I?"

"Yes," he replied.

"And you won't be -"

"I said I'll do it!" he hissed. "I don't have to like it, just... let me get it over with."

"I'll be inside," she continued, kissing him on the cheek before heading back into the house. "Just remember that you're doing the right thing."

Still looking across the garden, the original Mia heard the back door swinging shut. She briefly considered crying out for help, or trying to fight back, but deep down she still clung to the hope that this was part of some insane bluff, that David was about to tell her that he'd come up with a plan. With each passing second, however, that sense of confidence faded just a little more.

"Walk," he said, nudging her hard in the small of her back. "Let's not waste any time."

"I still can't get my head around this," she replied, stepping out across the lawn, heading toward the treeline at the far end. "It's like something from some kind of sci-fi film. Did that woman really come here from a parallel universe? What if there's some other explanation? What if she's a long-lost twin?"

She turned to him.

"David, what if -"

"Move!" he hissed, pushing her so hard that she almost fell over.

"David, you can't be serious about this," she continued, still hanging on desperately to the hope that he had a better plan. "David, you're my husband!"

"Can you turn around, please?" he asked. "Turn your back to me."

"Why?" she asked, glancing briefly at the knife in his hand before looking him in the eyes again. "What are you going to do?"

"Just turn around," he replied, conspicuously looking away from her slightly, as if he couldn't quite meet her gaze. "Don't make this any harder than it has to be."

"David -"

"She's you, okay?" he snapped suddenly, taking a step toward her with the knife raised. "In every conceivable way, that woman in there is you! She says that even a DNA test wouldn't be able to find any differences!"

"So what?"

"So she's you but -"

He caught himself just in time.

"But what?" she asked incredulously. "Better?"

"I didn't use that word," he told her.

"But you were thinking it," she continued, barely able to believe what she was hearing. "Are you out of your mind?"

"You have to admit that things haven't been great between us lately," he insisted. "We've been having problems. You haven't wanted to be intimate with me, and you've been letting certain things get sloppy around the house, and you haven't even seemed very happy! Let's be honest, Mia, even before Catherine was born you were struggling a bit with mental health and stuff like that. Meanwhile this other version of you shows up and she doesn't have any of those problems."

"She's a maniac!" she hissed. "She's a murderer!"

"That's just while she was resetting things," he replied. "She's just a murderer in a specific...

limited way."

"And you're going to go along with it?" she said, still struggling to believe what she was hearing. "Are you actually willing to kill me in cold blood, just so that you can run off with this... improved version?"

She waited for an answer.

"Please turn around," he said finally, his voice trembling with emotion as tears filled his eyes. "Cooperate a little, Mia, and this can all be over in the blink of an eye. It only has to get messy and stabby and screamy if you insist on making it that way. I'm so sorry, but killing you is the only way to make our family perfect."

CHAPTER TWENTY-EIGHT

"WHAT ABOUT..."

She hesitated, still trying frantically to think of a way out; she had the basis of a plan forming in her head, even if she couldn't quite believe that it might ever work.

"What about one last reminder of what we had together?" she asked finally.

"What are you -"

"Just you and me," she continued, reaching out and touching the front of his trousers. "A comparison, if you like."

"Mia -"

"I know you've been fucking her," she sneered. "Don't even try to lie to me, because I know. So why don't you and I try one last time to rekindle that old spirit we used to have? You're willing to give me that, aren't you?" She hesitated, before slowly getting down onto her knees. "You won't even have to do anything," she added, looking up at him. "Isn't it only fair to let me try one last time? I want to show you that I can be as good as her. Just let me try my best to remind you."

"I don't know if that's strictly appropriate," he said, glancing over his shoulder to make sure that they couldn't be overheard. After a moment he looked down at her again. "I don't think she'd like it," he continued, lowering his voice to a conspiratorial whisper. "It doesn't feel right."

"What could be better than having one wife?" she asked. "How about two? Two versions of the same woman who can love you. Who can tend to your every need. Who can make love to you." She kept her gaze fixed on him. "Even at the same time. You always wanted to try a threesome, didn't you? Would it count if both the women were me?"

"I'm not sure that... this is going to work," he said awkwardly.

"She's me, and I'm her," she pointed out. "It's not even cheating, David. Technically we're the same woman in any kind of legal sense, so no court in the land could even accuse you of anything. I mean, that's the logic you're going with, isn't it? You think that if you kill me, there'll still be a version of me around so it'll be like you never did anything bad at all." She began to unzip the front of his trousers. "Doesn't the same logic apply here?"

He opened his mouth to reply, and then he flinched as he felt her reaching into his trousers and touching his manhood. After a moment she slipped it out into the open, and he sighed as he looked over his shoulder again. He could already feel himself getting hard.

"This is a very messed-up situation," he said under his breath. "I really don't get how I'm supposed to make sense of it all."

"Then don't try," she purred, staring straight ahead and starting to gently stroke him. "You're right, this *is* a messed-up situation." She moved her lips closer. "And I suppose we should do whatever it takes," she added, blowing gently, "to find a way to put it all right. But imagine having both of us in bed with you, competing to show you the best time. Wouldn't that be your ultimate fantasy?"

She looked up at him.

"Asshole!"

Before he could reach, she punched him as hard as she could manage in his undercarriage, almost forcing his testicles back up into his body. She grabbed his manhood and pulled him down, before elbowing him hard in the face and then pulling the knife from his hand. As he tried to force her back, she turned the knife around and briefly considered stabbing him, but at the last second she reconsidered; raising her arm, she watched for a moment as he tried to sit up, and then she smacked her elbow against one side of his forehead, knocking him out instantly.

"Sorry," she said breathlessly, getting to her feet while holding the knife in her trembling right hand and looking back toward the house, "but the real Mia's showing up again. And I'm taking back what's mine."

***

"You're *so* beautiful," the other Mia cooed softly, sitting in the dining room and cradling Catherine in her arms, trying to rock her to sleep. "Don't worry, Daddy'll be back inside soon and then we can all be a happy family again. That's all we've ever wanted, isn't it? To be together."

Hearing footsteps approaching the back door and stepping into the house, she smiled and turned to look over her shoulder.

"Hey, Daddy," she said with a grin, "what -"

Suddenly one of the spare paving slabs from outside slammed against the back of her head, sending her slumping forward. She let out a groggy cry, but she was powerless to resist as she felt Catherine being lifted from her arms; she turned and tried to grab the child, only to slump from the chair and land with a thud on the floor. Struggling to remain conscious, she found that her vision was slightly blurred as she looked up and saw a dark shape moving in front of the light; she blinked a couple of times, and finally she was able to see the original Mia stepping back with Catherine in her arms.

"What... what are..."

Her voice trailed off as she realized that she was struggling to keep from passing out. Reaching up, she touched the back of her head and felt sticky blood on her scalp, already mixing with her hair.

In the other Mia's arms, meanwhile, Catherine was starting to cry frantically.

"Give her back," the new Mia gasped, struggling very slowly to get to her feet. "She's mine now! Listen to her, she's crying because you hurt me!"

"She's not your baby!" the first Mia hissed. "She never was and she never will be!"

"How did you get back in here, anyway?" the new Mia asked, rubbing the back of her head and feeling more blood. "Damn it, I should have known David wouldn't be able to go through with the job I gave him. That was always his problem, at least back in my old world. He's a brilliant man, but he's held back by this overheated sense of honor. That's admirable, truly, but there are times when it rather gets in the way. Tell me, did you kill him or did you merely knock him out?"

"It was a bit of a low blow," she replied. "I've always known his weaknesses."

"Sex? Seriously, did you manage to overpower him by getting him horny?"

"Sounds like he's consistent, at least."

"I'm sure he'll crawl back in eventually," the new Mia continued, taking a step forward. "He's just -"

"Don't come any closer!" the first Mia yelled, holding up David's knife in her trembling left hand. "You're a monster!"

"I'm you."

"No," the first Mia said, shaking her head as she once again struggled to hold back tears. "No, you're nothing like me. Even if I believed that we started out the same – and I'm not saying that I *do* believe that, by the way – but even if I did, then we're definitely not the same now. You've obviously changed. You've become evil."

"I've been impacted by my life experiences, that's true," the new Mia replied. "I suppose the two biggest changes were David's life choices, and the fact that in my universe the IVF didn't work. Do you have any idea how lucky you are in this world, Mia? Do you have any idea how many worlds we looked at, searching for one where we had a child? We found hundreds of thousands, millions even, where we were denied that luck. How does it feel to be the only one who was blessed with success?

How does it feel to be the luckiest Mia Rush in all of existence? To be holding the only Catherine?"

"It feels like something worth defending," the first Mia told her.

"I don't blame you," the other Mia said. "You *should* fight. If you didn't fight, I'd start to wonder what's wrong with you. I'd start to think that you're not really me at all."

"I don't want to hurt you," the first Mia continued. "I don't want to hurt anyone."

"I can't go back where I came from. I knew it was going to be a one-way trip, right from the start. I suppose someone here could figure out what my David built, but I'm not exactly going to hold my breath." She took another step forward. "When I came here," she added, conspicuously keeping her eyes fixed on Catherine now, "I made a commitment."

"Too bad," the original Mia replied, "because that makes you surplus to requirements."

"Perhaps," the other Mia said, before taking a knife that had been left on the counter, "but the way I see it, you and I should be pretty much equal. We have the same instincts, we're roughly the same weight, and I think we're more or less at the same level of fitness. I suppose the real differentiator is going to be... who wants it more? Who wants Catherine more?"

"That's not even in question."

"Words are cheap," the other Mia said. "It's going to be actions that settle this. Now, the only real question is whether you're going to put Catherine down before we get started. Please do, I'd hate to think of her getting hurt. You wouldn't be thinking of using her as some kind of human shield, would you?"

"How dare you?" the original Mia replied, before setting Catherine in her crib and then stepping toward the middle of the room. She took a moment to settle her properly before turning to her double. "You really don't understand me at all, do you?"

"Please, I think I have a great deal of insight into both of us."

"Did you seriously think you could come here and steal my life?" the original Mia asked. "That's crazy, because in this universe at least, I'm pretty sure *I'd* never be so stupid or -"

Suddenly the other Mia lunged at her, screaming as she flashed the knife's blade toward her face.

CHAPTER TWENTY-NINE

LETTING OUT A FAINT groan, David blinked a couple of times before sitting up and finding himself out on the grass at the bottom of the garden. For a few seconds he couldn't remember how he'd ended up there, but then he looked back toward the house and the whole ridiculous tale flooded back into his mind.

"What..."

His voice trailed off as he realized that the house seemed completely still and quiet. He had no idea how long he'd been unconscious; morning hadn't come yet, but he heard no shouting or yelling, and no hint that the two Mias were fighting. He assumed that the original Mia – *his* Mia – would have gone back inside to get Catherine, and that neither of them would be willing to give up.

Hauling himself to his feet, he began to make his way along the path that led to the back door. He supposed that if the two Mias had fought, he could just be happy with whichever version was left over, although he knew that the original Mia might be a little angry. Still, he told himself that he could probably calm her down, and that it wasn't as if he'd cheated; he'd merely tried to make the best of a bad situation, and given the circumstances he thought that he'd not done a terrible job. Plus, if they were both in there, some kind of compromise might be possible.

Reaching the back door, he looked into the kitchen. To his horror, he saw one Mia standing over the other, holding a knife; she turned to him, and in that moment he had no idea which of them had won.

***

On the floor, one of the Mias had been tied up, with a thick gag covering her mouth. She tried to roll onto her back, only to find that she couldn't move; she tried to roll the other way, but again she was unable to shift at all. Finally she looked up at David and tried to scream, although the gag muffled her cries.

"It's her," the other Mia said, sounding exhausted as she limped over to the crib and began to lift Catherine up. "On the floor, I mean. It's not me. It's her."

The Mia on the floor tried again to cry out.

"That's the one who came here from... wherever," the other Mia said, holding Catherine gently in her arms. "I had to tie her up and gag her, to stop her going on and on about stuff. I couldn't kill her; neither of us could kill the other, I guess that's what she was talking about earlier."

David opened his mouth to reply, but at the last moment he hesitated.

"It's me!" Mia hissed. "Are you seriously suggesting that you don't know the difference?"

"I didn't say that," he replied quickly, and a little defensively. "I would never say that!"

"Last Christmas we went to that restaurant in Leicester Square and had the worst meal of our lives," she reminded him. "The year before we were at your parents' house and we had to listen to them squabbling all the time about the new air-fryer. The year before that, we were at that cottage in Wales with Jackie and Nick. Somehow I really don't think that the duplicate version of me would have done exactly the same thing at Christmas. Do you?"

She waited for an answer.

"*Do* you?" she snapped after a couple of seconds.

"No," he replied, shaking his head. "Absolutely not."

"So she's tied up," she continued, looking down at the struggling Mia on the floor, "but I don't know what to do with her now."

"Me neither," he said.

"Really? So you were perfectly willing to kill me, but you couldn't do the same thing to her?"

"You said -"

"I know what I said!" she hissed. "The point is that you were going to do it!"

"No, I wasn't," he insisted. "Absolutely not. I was going to walk you down to the bottom of the garden, so that you were out of sight of the house, and then I was going to... let you go." He waited for her to tell him that she believed his claim. "It's true! I admit that I didn't have a fully-formed plan, but I had enough of an idea to be getting on with. I was going to make her think that I'd done something bad, and that way I would have bought us some more time."

He paused, still waiting for her to say something.

"Honest!" he added finally.

"We need to put her somewhere," Mia muttered. "We can't let her go, and I don't really know what would happen if we went to the police. They'd probably think we're insane, and there could be complications. For a start, I'm sure they'd take Catherine away from us." She paused, watching as the other Mia continued to struggle on the floor.

"We could keep her in the basement," she added. "You know, the basement we didn't even know we had?"

"How long for?" he asked.

"I don't know. Forever?" She took a deep breath. "Until we figure this out, at least."

"And then what?"

"I don't know, David!" she snapped angrily. "Maybe she can be your weird alternate sex slave version of me! You can make her do all the sick stuff you wish I'd agree to do with you. You can have the nice version of me up here, making your dinner and looking after the house, and then you can have the depraved version of me down there in the basement letting you do butt stuff to her. Wouldn't that be your ideal life?"

"Would you really let me do that?"

"I was joking!" she shouted furiously, before kissing Catherine as the baby started to cry again. "Sorry, my little darling," she continued, "I was just being sarcastic about something and apparently your father thought it was a serious proposition."

"I didn't," David replied. "I knew you were joking."

"Get her into the basement," she continued, "and we'll go from there. I'm exhausted, and I've just been in an actual knife fight, and so much is going round and round in my head right now that I can barely keep my thoughts together. Tomorrow we'll have to sit down and figure out what we're going to do, and how we explain all this crap if we actually go to the police. I just can't handle all of that drama right now."

"Right," he said, before stepping over to the bound and gagged version of his wife on the floor. He stared at her for a few seconds, still trying to work out exactly what was going on. "And you're *sure* this is the interloper, aren't you?"

He turned to Mia and saw that she was glaring at him.

"Right," he continued, forcing a smile as he reached down and grabbed the other Mia's arm, before starting to drag her out of the kitchen as she tried desperately to break free from her restraints. "I'm just not going to think right now, okay? I'm not even going to try. When I think, things tend to go wrong." He adjusted his grip on the woman's arm before pulling her out into the hallway. "Don't worry, you can count on me from now on. I won't let anything bad happen. I'm going to protect our family."

"Like you did before?" she asked, rolling her eyes before looking down at Catherine again. "Sweetheart, I'm so sorry you had to go through all of this," she whispered. "It's like we've all been haunted by another version of Mummy, isn't it? Or I've been haunting her. We've been haunting each other in a way. Two hauntings for the price of one. At least you're too young to remember any of this. And I promise, hand on heart, that you're never going to find out that this happened. Never ever. I'll always make sure that it's kept from you, because something like this... something like this could really screw you up."

Wandering to the doorway, she looked through into the front room, just in time to see that David was in the process of manhandling the other version of herself and getting her down into the basement. After a moment, as the other woman's feet disappeared from view and were followed by a thud at the bottom of the steps, David looked up and met his wife's gaze, and for a few seconds he seemed to freeze in place, almost as if he'd been caught doing something wrong.

"Is everything okay over there?" Mia called out. "David? Are you sure I can trust you to do the right thing?"

"Of course," he stammered. "You know that. I love you, Mia. I know things have been a little rocky lately, but I really think we can put that in the past. After tonight... I truly believe that everything's going to be okay. We're going to be a happy family again. Everything's going to go back to normal."

"Put the alternate universe variant of me in the basement and make sure she can't escape," Mia replied. "Then I need to get some sleep for a few hours before we decide what we're going to do with her. And, hey, there's always a chance I might get lucky and find this was all just a nightmare."

CHAPTER THIRTY

SEVERAL HOURS LATER, HAVING tried but mostly failed to get some sleep, Mia Rush stepped out of her bedroom and pulled the door shut. David was snoring soundly, and Catherine was in her crib, but Mia felt as if she was still living in some kind of bizarre dream.

"It's going to be okay," she whispered, before making her way down the stairs. "Everything's going to be completely fine."

Feeling tired but wired at the same time, she walked like a zombie through to the kitchen. She had no real plan, but she'd spent too much time already trying to get back to sleep and she figured that she might as well get on with the day. She glanced at the clock on the oven and saw that the time was almost 7am, and then – as morning light streamed though the window – she began to head over to the counter, only to stop at the last moment as she spotted something sitting on the table in the corner.

Her breast pump.

"What the..."

Heading over, she looked down and saw that this was her old pump, the same one that had mysteriously vanished. She'd gone crazy looking for the damn thing, she'd almost ripped the house apart, yet now here it was back on the table in plain sight as if it had never gone away.

She looked round, but there was no sign of anyone else in the kitchen.

Picking the pump up, she tried to work out where it could possibly have been. All sorts of possibilities were running through her mind, but finally she told herself that somehow in all the madness it must have been misplaced; another possibility was that the crazy other version of herself had stolen it, although she had no idea why it would have been returned now. As she set it back down, she told herself that there was no reason to worry and that she certainly shouldn't start stressing about something so mundane.

"Welcome back," she said with a faint smile, before making her way over to the sink. "Wait there. I'm going to be needing you soon. It's time to start getting back to normal."

***

The clock on the oven ticked over to quarter past seven.

Taking a seat at the table, with a steaming cup of coffee nearby, Mia took a deep breath and told herself that she really needed to try to get back to normal. Sure, a crazed variant of herself from another universe might be tied up in the basement, but somehow she'd started to get used to weird events. In the back of her mind she knew that she and David were going to have to go to the police, and she figured that eventually they'd just have to believe their story; she knew there'd be a lot of questioning, especially about Jackie and Nick, but she told herself that they had all the evidence they needed.

Eventually the police would have to understand.

She took a sip of coffee and immediately felt much better. As she set the cup down, she spotted the breast pump again, and she realized that more than anything else in the whole world she just wanted to forget all the madness. She hadn't expressed for a while, and while she wasn't sure that she was quite in the mood, finally she slid the pump closer before pulling her shirt aside and exposing one breast.

"I'm your mummy," she muttered, thinking of Catherine fast asleep upstairs, "not that... hag from another world."

She attached the pump to her breast and then took another sip of coffee. Hearing a noise outside, she looked over at the window just in time to see a starling landing on a tree branch outside. For a few seconds, with the pump attached to her breast and ready to go, she actually allowed herself to believe that normality was returning, and that she and David and Catherine had a chance to get back to how things had always been. The starling hopped along the branch for a few seconds before flying off, and a smile crossed Mia's lips as she realized that the rest of the world was still running along as normal.

Grabbing the handle on the pump, she pulled it down, ready to produce the first milk.

Suddenly she screamed as she felt an immense pain ripping through her breast. She pulled her hand away, but the pump remained firmly attached to her chest and after a moment blood began to dribble through into the jar. Letting out a shocked gasp, she saw small pieces of flesh in the blood, and when she tried to move the pump away she found that it had gouged into her breast and had begun to mince the tip, including the nipple. She pulled a little harder, trying to ignore the pain, but strands of skin and meat were firmly caught in a set of metal teeth that had somehow been attached to the inside of the pump.

"Please," she stammered, "don't -"

"Calm down!" a voice hissed, as hands reached around from behind her and took hold of the pump. More blood was running freely into the jar. "It's just a little adjustment I made a while ago."

Looking up, Mia saw to her horror that the other version of herself was leaning over her shoulder. Hearing a bumping sound, she looked over at the doorway and saw David watching, although after a moment he stepped out of view.

"David!" she gasped. "Don't -"

The other Mia pulled the pump's handle down, and metal teeth chewed through almost an entire half of the breast, letting the torn chunks drop down into the bottle.

"Careful," the other Mia purred, leaning over a little more so that she could get a better view, "I really went to town on this. I've always had a slight flair for the dramatic, and I had a lot of time to daydream while I watched my David work. Now, let's see..."

She pulled the handle again, feeding more of Mia's tattered breast into the pump. Letting out a cry of pain, the original Mia reached out and steadied herself against the table, but a moment later the other Mia pulled the handle yet again; this time, along with meat from the breast, several ribs were ripped out of place and pulled into the teeth; fragments of bone fell through into the container.

"It's *very* powerful," the other Mia explained. "I know I said I couldn't hurt you, and that's true. Sort of. I couldn't attack you in any knowing way, but somehow this is different. All I'm doing is helping you to express a little milk, and it's really not my fault if someone rigged the pump earlier. Turns out, random acts of aggression are off the cards, but I can find ways to... trick the system. Gotta love a loophole, right?"

"Stop!" Mia gasped, trying once again to pull herself free, even as she felt her rib-cage starting to crack. "Please..."

"David let me out again," the other Mia continued. "I must admit, the changes I made to this pump have exceeded even my own lofty expectations. Don't you think there's something just so satisfying about a plan that comes together so perfectly?" She pulled the handle yet again, and this time the original Mia screamed as she felt more bones shattering in her chest. "It didn't have to be like this, you know," the other Mia said. "You really forced the issue, when we could have cooperated instead. Then again, I should have known how stubborn you'd be. Aren't we just two peas in the same pod?"

"Please," the original Mia gasped, as more blood dribbled into the container, "don't do this. I just want to look after my daughter, that's all. I just want to keep her safe."

"She's going to be just fine," the other Mia said. "My maternal instincts have really begun to kick in. As for you, I think you just need to focus on the positives rather than always dwelling on things that can go wrong."

She tightened her grip on the pump as the original Mia sobbed frantically.

"We're the same, you and I," the other Mia told her. "That's a good thing. And I know you can do this, I really do. It shouldn't even be too hard." She tightened her grip again. "Really... you've just to put your heart into it."

With that, she pumped again. This time the metal teeth ripped out more ribs and pulled Mia's heart from her chest, running it through the mincer and sending the hot throbbing pieces clattering into the jaw as the original Mia let out a pained scream and drew her final breath.

***

Holding his daughter in his arms, David stepped into the doorway and looked into the kitchen. He immediately flinched as he saw Mia standing in the middle of the room, soaked in blood.

Behind her, more blood was dribbling off the side of the table, while a body lay on the floor.

"It's okay," Mia said, her eyes glistening with tears as a smile spread across her face. Stepping forward, she reached out and took little Catherine from her husband's arms. "There's no need to be scared. Mummy's here now."

EPILOGUE

"MUMMY'S HERE," MIA RUSH said a week later, as she held Catherine latch on. "There you go. Take as much as you want."

"And you're really producing milk now?" David said, watching from behind the counter. "How does that work, exactly?"

"It's just my maternal instinct kicking in," Mia explained. "I don't think that's something a man could ever truly understand. Somewhere deep inside me, some part of my body recognizes that my daughter needs feeding, so various processes kick into gear. And the result is that everyone's happy."

"Is it... healthy?"

"What do you mean?"

"I mean, is it healthy for her to drink that?"

"I'm her mother," she pointed out. "This is

the most natural thing in the world. Besides, you've tried some direct from the source and you didn't complain."

"She certainly seems fine," David admitted, watching for a moment as his daughter continued to feed. He was clearly in awe at the whole situation, but after a moment he simply shook his head as if he'd accepted that he would never quite get it all sorted in his mind. "You're right, I don't think I quite understand, but that's okay. I don't think I really need to." He paused for a moment. "And is everything else okay?" he asked cautiously. "I know this is going to sound crazy, but I just feel like it's all been too easy. There should have been -"

"Stop worrying," Mia said firmly. "What could go wrong? Do you think anyone's going to report me missing? I'm not missing! I'm right here!"

"Sure," he replied, "but what about Nick?"

"The police seemed to believe our statement about him not coming here," she continued. "Besides, why would anyone ever think that we'd hurt your best friend in all the world? I get it, David, you're worried but... I promise you, everything's fine now. We've dealt with the... slight problem that occurred. She's resting in peace now, which is the best thing for her after all the trouble she went through."

She watched him for a moment, while slowly growing a little more concerned.

"You're not worried, are you?" she asked.

"Me?" He thought about that question for a moment. "No, not at all."

"And you don't..."

Her voice trailed off for a moment, as Catherine continued to feed.

"You don't *miss* her, do you?"

"Of course not."

"Because that would be ridiculous," she continued. "I'm her, in every conceivable way. Sure, I don't have her memories, but otherwise there's absolutely no difference. I know the David in my world would never have been silly about all of this. You're not going to be silly, are you?"

"Me? Never." He hesitated, and he still seemed a little unconvinced. "I have to go and check on some work things, though," he added, heading out of the room. "You'll be okay here, won't you?"

"Of course we will," she replied, looking down at Catherine and smiling with absolute, genuine pleasure. "How could we not be? We're just a mother and her daughter, doing the most natural thing in the whole wide world."

***

"There you go," Mia said a while later, as she reached into the crib and set Catherine down. "You must be tired after such a long day. Why don't you get a nice nap?"

Catherine gurgled happily.

"You're my special little girl," Mia continued, tickling the side of her face. "You'll *always* be my special little girl. Do you have any idea how much trouble I went to, just to get here and be with you? I crossed universes to find you, my sweet darling, because I always knew deep in my heart that you were around somewhere. I just felt it in here." She touched her chest. "Where it matters."

For a moment she could only stare at Catherine, wrapped up in a sense of wonder; she wanted to freeze time, to keep her as a baby forever, yet at the same time she was also desperate to see her grow and develop. More than anything, she wanted to keep her safe, and she told herself that she was going to be the best child any mother had ever known. Catherine would want for nothing, need for nothing, beg for nothing; she was going to be happy and content, and nourished, and she would have every possible opportunity. She wouldn't know pain or hunger or sadness or longing, or any of those other bad feelings that could open cracks in a soul.

"I've got you," she said finally. "Now and forever, I've -"

Before she could finish, she heard a loud

bump coming from upstairs. She looked at the ceiling; she knew David had popped out for a few hours, and that she and Catherine were alone, but the bump had seemed very sudden. A moment later she heard a shuffling sound, following by what seemed to be the sound of a door creaking open. Puzzled, she made her way out into the hallway and looked at the stairs, but already she could feel a sense of concern starting to spread through her chest. She opened her mouth to call out, but she stopped herself just in time.

Glancing back at the crib, she realized that her heart was racing, but she tried to focus on the thought that she was simply overreacting.

"Sweetheart, wait there," she said cautiously, even though she knew Catherine was too young to understand. "Mummy's just going to..."

She turned to look at the staircase again.

"Check on something."

Heading to the stairs, she stopped briefly to listen before making her way up. She told herself over and over again that she was imagining things, that there was no reason to worry, and as she reached the landing she saw that nothing seemed to be amiss. So far, so good, but when she walked over to the spare bedroom and looked inside, she spotted what appeared to be a kind of burn pattern on the wallpaper in the corner. She headed over to take a look; rubbing her hand gently against the darkened patch, she felt that the paper was slightly mottled and blistered, and warm as well, almost as if...

"No," she whispered, "that's not possible. There can't be another one."

She looked around the room, and although she saw no-one now, she couldn't shake the feeling that she was being watched. Or, if not watched, then at least monitored.

Suddenly she heard another bump coming from one of the other bedrooms. She looked toward the landing, just in time to hear more footsteps shuffling across a nearby carpet. Hurrying to the door, she leaned out, but now the footsteps had stopped. She made her way to the master bedroom, and she froze as soon as she saw another burned, mottled effect on the wall near the dresser. Stepping closer, she touched this patch, and sure enough she found that it too was still slightly warm.

"No," she said firmly, "there can't be any more of -"

She flinched as she heard a third bump, this time coming from the landing, followed by a scraping sound. Hurrying out, she saw yet another dark patch on the wall, and the small table at the top of the stairs had been pushed aside as if something had forced its way out from the wall itself. Making her way over, she touched the wall and yet again discovered a warm patch.

"This can't be happening," she said through

gritted teeth. "She's mine. She's all mine and -"

Another bump rang out, this time coming from the attic. She looked up, but then she turned to look at the stairs as she heard another bump coming from one of the lower rooms; then, hearing another bump coming from the spare bedroom, she looked across the landing. Now there was a new bump every few seconds, and the sound of scurrying footsteps seemed to be ringing out from all around the house.

"She's mine," Mia stammered again, filled with a growing sense of panic. "Please..."

As she stood on the landing, she heard more and more bumping sounds, and more and more whispers of footsteps. She spotted a hint of movement in the master bedroom, just a shadow moving across one of the walls, followed by the sound of someone walking across the attic above; moments later she realized she could hear voices somewhere far off, accompanied moments later by a hissing sound and several more thuds, as if two people were fighting in one of the rooms. Downstairs, footsteps were criss-crossing the rooms, and a moment later she heard Catherine starting to let out a series of gurgles.

"No!" Mia screamed, as she heard more and more thuds coming from every room in the house, and more sets of footsteps and more whispers. "Go away! You can't have her! I got here first!"

Also by Amy Cross

1689
(The Haunting of Hadlow House book 1)

All Richard Hadlow wants is a happy family and a peaceful home. Having built the perfect house deep in the Kent countryside, now all he needs is a wife. He's about to discover, however, that even the most perfectly-laid plans can go horribly and tragically wrong.

The year is 1689 and England is in the grip of turmoil. A pretender is trying to take the throne, but Richard has no interest in the affairs of his country. He only cares about finding the perfect wife and giving her a perfect life. But someone – or something – at his newly-built house has other ideas. Is Richard's new life about to be destroyed forever?

Hadlow House is brand new, but already there are strange whispers in the corridors and unexplained noises at night. Has Richard been unlucky, is his new wife simply imagining things, or is a dark secret from the past about to rise up and deliver Richard's worst nightmare? Who wins when the past and the present collide?

Also by Amy Cross

The Haunting of Nelson Street
(The Ghosts of Crowford book 1)

Crowford, a sleepy coastal town in the south of England, might seem like an oasis of calm and tranquility. Beneath the surface, however, dark secrets are waiting to claim fresh victims, and ghostly figures plot revenge.

Having finally decided to leave the hustle of London, Daisy and Richard Johnson buy two houses on Nelson Street, a picturesque street in the center of Crowford. One house is perfect and ready to move into, while the other is a fire-ravaged wreck that needs a lot of work. They figure they have plenty of time to work on the damaged house while Daisy recovers from a traumatic event.

Soon, they discover that the two houses share a common link to the past. Something awful once happened on Nelson Street, something that shook the town to its core.

Also by Amy Cross

The Revenge of the Mercy Belle
(The Ghosts of Crowford book 2)

The year is 1950, and a great tragedy has struck the town of Crowford. Three local men have been killed in a storm, after their fishing boat the Mercy Belle sank. A mysterious fourth man, however, was rescue. Nobody knows who he is, or what he was doing on the Mercy Belle... and the man has lost his memory.

Five years later, messages from the dead warn of impending doom for Crowford. The ghosts of the Mercy Belle's crew demand revenge, and the whole town is being punished. The fourth man still has no memory of his previous existence, but he's married now and living under the named Edward Smith. As Crowford's suffering continues, the locals begin to turn against him.

What really happened on the night the Mercy Belle sank? Did the fourth man cause the tragedy? And will Crowford survive if this man is not sent to meet his fate?

Also by Amy Cross

The Devil, the Witch and the Whore
(The Deal book 1)

"Leave the forest alone. Whatever's out there, just let it be. Don't make it angry."

When a horrific discovery is made at the edge of town, Sheriff James Kopperud realizes the answers he seeks might be waiting beyond in the vast forest. But everybody in the town of Deal knows that there's something out there in the forest, something that should never be disturbed. A deal was made long ago, a deal that was supposed to keep the town safe. And if he insists on investigating the murder of a local girl, James is going to have to break that deal and head out into the wilderness.

Meanwhile, James has no idea that his estranged daughter Ramsey has returned to town. Ramsey is running from something, and she thinks she can find safety in the vast tunnel system that runs beneath the forest. Before long, however, Ramsey finds herself coming face to face with creatures that hide in the shadows. One of these creatures is known as the devil, and another is known as the witch. They're both waiting for the whore to arrive, but for very different reasons. And soon Ramsey is offered a terrible deal, one that could save or destroy the entire town, and maybe even the world.

Also by Amy Cross

The Soul Auction

"I saw a woman on the beach. I watched her face a demon."

Thirty years after her mother's death, Alice Ashcroft is drawn back to the coastal English town of Curridge. Somebody in Curridge has been reviewing Alice's novels online, and in those reviews there have been tantalizing hints at a hidden truth. A truth that seems to be linked to her dead mother.

"Thirty years ago, there was a soul auction."

Once she reaches Curridge, Alice finds strange things happening all around her. Something attacks her car. A figure watches her on the beach at night. And when she tries to find the person who has been reviewing her books, she makes a horrific discovery.

What really happened to Alice's mother thirty years ago? Who was she talking to, just moments before dropping dead on the beach? What caused a huge rockfall that nearly tore a nearby cliff-face in half? And what sinister presence is lurking in the grounds of the local church?

Also by Amy Cross

Darper Danver: The Complete First Series

Five years ago, three friends went to a remote cabin in the woods and tried to contact the spirit of a long-dead soldier. They thought they could control whatever happened next. They were wrong...

Newly released from prison, Cassie Briggs returns to Fort Powell, determined to get her life back on track. Soon, however, she begins to suspect that an ancient evil still lurks in the nearby cabin. Was the mysterious Darper Danver really destroyed all those years ago, or does her spirit still linger, waiting for a chance to return?

As Cassie and her ex-boyfriend Fisher are finally forced to face the truth about what happened in the cabin, they realize that Darper isn't ready to let go of their lives just yet. Meanwhile, a vengeful woman plots revenge for her brother's murder, and a New York ghost writer arrives in town to uncover the truth. Before long, strange carvings begin to appear around town and blood starts to flow once again.

AMY CROSS

Also by Amy Cross

The Ghost of Molly Holt

"Molly Holt is dead. There's nothing to fear in this house."

When three teenagers set out to explore an abandoned house in the middle of a forest, they think they've found the location where the infamous Molly Holt video was filmed.

They've found much more than that...

Tim doesn't believe in ghosts, but he has a crush on a girl who does. That's why he ends up taking her out to the house, and it's also why he lets her take his only flashlight. But as they explore the house together, Tim and Becky start to realize that something else might be lurking in the shadows.

Something that, ten years ago, suffered unimaginable pain.

Something that won't rest until a terrible wrong has been put right.

Also by Amy Cross

American Coven

He kidnapped three women and held them in his basement. He thought they couldn't fight back. He was wrong...

Snatched from the street near her home, Holly Carter is taken to a rural house and thrown down into a stone basement. She meets two other women who have also been kidnapped, and soon Holly learns about the horrific rituals that take place in the house. Eventually, she's called upstairs to take her place in the ice bath.

As her nightmare continues, however, Holly learns about a mysterious power that exists in the basement, and which the three women might be able to harness. When they finally manage to get through the metal door, however, the women have no idea that their fight for freedom is going to stretch out for more than a decade, or that it will culminate in a final, devastating demonstration of their new-found powers.

Also by Amy Cross

The Ash House

Why would anyone ever return to a haunted house?

For Diane Mercer the answer is simple. She's dying of cancer, and she wants to know once and for all whether ghosts are real.

Heading home with her young son, Diane is determined to find out whether the stories are real. After all, everyone else claimed to see and hear strange things in the house over the years. Everyone except Diane had some kind of experience in the house, or in the little ash house in the yard.

As Diane explores the house where she grew up, however, her son is exploring the yard and the forest. And while his mother might be struggling to come to terms with her own impending death, Daniel Mercer is puzzled by fleeting appearances of a strange little girl who seems drawn to the ash house, and by strange, rasping coughs that he keeps hearing at night.

The Ash House is a horror novel about a woman who desperately wants to know what will happen to her when she dies, and about a boy who uncovers the shocking truth about a young girl's murder.

AMY CROSS

Also by Amy Cross

Haunted

Twenty years ago, the ghost of a dead little girl drove Sheriff Michael Blaine to his death.

Now, that same ghost is coming for his daughter.

Returning to the small town where she grew up, Alex Roberts is determined to live a normal, quiet life. For the residents of Railham, however, she's an unwelcome reminder of the town's darkest hour.

Twenty years ago, nine-year-old Mo Garvey was found brutally murdered in a nearby forest. Everyone thinks that Alex's father was responsible, but if the killer was brought to justice, why is the ghost of Mo Garvey still after revenge?

And how far will the real killer go to protect his secret, when Alex starts getting closer to the truth?

Haunted is a horror novel about a woman who has to face her past, about a town that would rather forget, and about a little girl who refuses to let death stand in her way.

AMY CROSS

Also by Amy Cross

The Curse of Wetherley House

"If you walk through that door, Evil Mary will get you."

When she agrees to visit a supposedly haunted house with an old friend, Rosie assumes she'll encounter nothing more scary than a few creaks and bumps in the night. Even the legend of Evil Mary doesn't put her off. After all, she knows ghosts aren't real. But when Mary makes her first appearance, Rosie realizes she might already be trapped.

For more than a century, Wetherley House has been cursed. A horrific encounter on a remote road in the late 1800's has already caused a chain of misery and pain for all those who live at the house. Wetherley House was abandoned long ago, after a terrible discovery in the basement, something has remained undetected within its room. And even the local children know that Evil Mary waits in the house for anyone foolish enough to walk through the front door.

Before long, Rosie realizes that her entire life has been defined by the spirit of a woman who died in agony. Can she become the first person to escape Evil Mary, or will she fall victim to the same fate as the house's other occupants?

AMY CROSS

Also by Amy Cross

The Girl Who Never Came Back

Twenty years ago, Charlotte Abernathy vanished while playing near her family's house. Despite a frantic search, no trace of her was found until a year later, when the little girl turned up on the doorstep with no memory of where she'd been.

Today, Charlotte has put her mysterious ordeal behind her, even though she's never learned where she was during that missing year. However, when her eight-year-old niece vanishes in similar circumstances, a fully-grown Charlotte is forced to make a fresh attempt to uncover the truth.

Originally published in 2013, the fully revised and updated version of *The Girl Who Never Came Back* tells the harrowing story of a woman who thought she could forget her past, and of a little girl caught in the tangled web of a dark family secret.

AMY CROSS

BOOKS BY AMY CROSS

1. Dark Season: The Complete First Series (2011)
2. Werewolves of Soho (Lupine Howl book 1) (2012)
3. Werewolves of the Other London (Lupine Howl book 2) (2012)
4. Ghosts: The Complete Series (2012)
5. Dark Season: The Complete Second Series (2012)
6. The Children of Black Annis (Lupine Howl book 3) (2012)
7. Destiny of the Last Wolf (Lupine Howl book 4) (2012)
8. Asylum (The Asylum Trilogy book 1) (2012)
9. Dark Season: The Complete Third Series (2013)
10. Devil's Briar (2013)
11. Broken Blue (The Broken Trilogy book 1) (2013)
12. The Night Girl (2013)
13. Days 1 to 4 (Mass Extinction Event book 1) (2013)
14. Days 5 to 8 (Mass Extinction Event book 2) (2013)
15. The Library (The Library Chronicles book 1) (2013)
16. American Coven (2013)
17. Werewolves of Sangreth (Lupine Howl book 5) (2013)
18. Broken White (The Broken Trilogy book 2) (2013)
19. Grave Girl (Grave Girl book 1) (2013)
20. Other People's Bodies (2013)
21. The Shades (2013)
22. The Vampire's Grave and Other Stories (2013)
23. Darper Danver: The Complete First Series (2013)
24. The Hollow Church (2013)
25. The Dead and the Dying (2013)
26. Days 9 to 16 (Mass Extinction Event book 3) (2013)
27. The Girl Who Never Came Back (2013)
28. Ward Z (The Ward Z Series book 1) (2013)
29. Journey to the Library (The Library Chronicles book 2) (2014)
30. The Vampires of Tor Cliff Asylum (2014)
31. The Family Man (2014)
32. The Devil's Blade (2014)
33. The Immortal Wolf (Lupine Howl book 6) (2014)
34. The Dying Streets (Detective Laura Foster book 1) (2014)
35. The Stars My Home (2014)
36. The Ghost in the Rain and Other Stories (2014)
37. Ghosts of the River Thames (The Robinson Chronicles book 1) (2014)
38. The Wolves of Cur'eath (2014)
39. Days 46 to 53 (Mass Extinction Event book 4) (2014)
40. The Man Who Saw the Face of the World (2014)
41. The Art of Dying (Detective Laura Foster book 2) (2014)
42. Raven Revivals (Grave Girl book 2) (2014)

AMY CROSS

43. Arrival on Thaxos (Dead Souls book 1) (2014)
44. Birthright (Dead Souls book 2) (2014)
45. A Man of Ghosts (Dead Souls book 3) (2014)
46. The Haunting of Hardstone Jail (2014)
47. A Very Respectable Woman (2015)
48. Better the Devil (2015)
49. The Haunting of Marshall Heights (2015)
50. Terror at Camp Everbee (The Ward Z Series book 2) (2015)
51. Guided by Evil (Dead Souls book 4) (2015)
52. Child of a Bloodied Hand (Dead Souls book 5) (2015)
53. Promises of the Dead (Dead Souls book 6) (2015)
54. Days 54 to 61 (Mass Extinction Event book 5) (2015)
55. Angels in the Machine (The Robinson Chronicles book 2) (2015)
56. The Curse of Ah-Qal's Tomb (2015)
57. Broken Red (The Broken Trilogy book 3) (2015)
58. The Farm (2015)
59. Fallen Heroes (Detective Laura Foster book 3) (2015)
60. The Haunting of Emily Stone (2015)
61. Cursed Across Time (Dead Souls book 7) (2015)
62. Destiny of the Dead (Dead Souls book 8) (2015)
63. The Death of Jennifer Kazakos (Dead Souls book 9) (2015)
64. Alice Isn't Well (Death Herself book 1) (2015)
65. Annie's Room (2015)
66. The House on Everley Street (Death Herself book 2) (2015)
67. Meds (The Asylum Trilogy book 2) (2015)
68. Take Me to Church (2015)
69. Ascension (Demon's Grail book 1) (2015)
70. The Priest Hole (Nykolas Freeman book 1) (2015)
71. Eli's Town (2015)
72. The Horror of Raven's Briar Orphanage (Dead Souls book 10) (2015)
73. The Witch of Thaxos (Dead Souls book 11) (2015)
74. The Rise of Ashalla (Dead Souls book 12) (2015)
75. Evolution (Demon's Grail book 2) (2015)
76. The Island (The Island book 1) (2015)
77. The Lighthouse (2015)
78. The Cabin (The Cabin Trilogy book 1) (2015)
79. At the Edge of the Forest (2015)
80. The Devil's Hand (2015)
81. The 13th Demon (Demon's Grail book 3) (2016)
82. After the Cabin (The Cabin Trilogy book 2) (2016)
83. The Border: The Complete Series (2016)
84. The Dead Ones (Death Herself book 3) (2016)
85. A House in London (2016)
86. Persona (The Island book 2) (2016)

87. Battlefield (Nykolas Freeman book 2) (2016)
88. Perfect Little Monsters and Other Stories (2016)
89. The Ghost of Shapley Hall (2016)
90. The Blood House (2016)
91. The Death of Addie Gray (2016)
92. The Girl With Crooked Fangs (2016)
93. Last Wrong Turn (2016)
94. The Body at Auercliff (2016)
95. The Printer From Hell (2016)
96. The Dog (2016)
97. The Nurse (2016)
98. The Haunting of Blackwych Grange (2016)
99. Twisted Little Things and Other Stories (2016)
100. The Horror of Devil's Root Lake (2016)
101. The Disappearance of Katie Wren (2016)
102. B&B (2016)
103. The Bride of Ashbyrn House (2016)
104. The Devil, the Witch and the Whore (The Deal Trilogy book 1) (2016)
105. The Ghosts of Lakeforth Hotel (2016)
106. The Ghost of Longthorn Manor and Other Stories (2016)
107. Laura (2017)
108. The Murder at Skellin Cottage (Jo Mason book 1) (2017)
109. The Curse of Wetherley House (2017)
110. The Ghosts of Hexley Airport (2017)
111. The Return of Rachel Stone (Jo Mason book 2) (2017)
112. Haunted (2017)
113. The Vampire of Downing Street and Other Stories (2017)
114. The Ash House (2017)
115. The Ghost of Molly Holt (2017)
116. The Camera Man (2017)
117. The Soul Auction (2017)
118. The Abyss (The Island book 3) (2017)
119. Broken Window (The House of Jack the Ripper book 1) (2017)
120. In Darkness Dwell (The House of Jack the Ripper book 2) (2017)
121. Cradle to Grave (The House of Jack the Ripper book 3) (2017)
122. The Lady Screams (The House of Jack the Ripper book 4) (2017)
123. A Beast Well Tamed (The House of Jack the Ripper book 5) (2017)
124. Doctor Charles Grazier (The House of Jack the Ripper book 6) (2017)
125. The Raven Watcher (The House of Jack the Ripper book 7) (2017)
126. The Final Act (The House of Jack the Ripper book 8) (2017)
127. Stephen (2017)
128. The Spider (2017)
129. The Mermaid's Revenge (2017)
130. The Girl Who Threw Rocks at the Devil (2018)

131. Friend From the Internet (2018)
132. Beautiful Familiar (2018)
133. One Night at a Soul Auction (2018)
134. 16 Frames of the Devil's Face (2018)
135. The Haunting of Caldgrave House (2018)
136. Like Stones on a Crow's Back (The Deal Trilogy book 2) (2018)
137. Room 9 and Other Stories (2018)
138. The Gravest Girl of All (Grave Girl book 3) (2018)
139. Return to Thaxos (Dead Souls book 13) (2018)
140. The Madness of Annie Radford (The Asylum Trilogy book 3) (2018)
141. The Haunting of Briarwych Church (Briarwych book 1) (2018)
142. I Just Want You To Be Happy (2018)
143. Day 100 (Mass Extinction Event book 6) (2018)
144. The Horror of Briarwych Church (Briarwych book 2) (2018)
145. The Ghost of Briarwych Church (Briarwych book 3) (2018)
146. Lights Out (2019)
147. Apocalypse (The Ward Z Series book 3) (2019)
148. Days 101 to 108 (Mass Extinction Event book 7) (2019)
149. The Haunting of Daniel Bayliss (2019)
150. The Purchase (2019)
151. Harper's Hotel Ghost Girl (Death Herself book 4) (2019)
152. The Haunting of Aldburn House (2019)
153. Days 109 to 116 (Mass Extinction Event book 8) (2019)
154. Bad News (2019)
155. The Wedding of Rachel Blaine (2019)
156. Dark Little Wonders and Other Stories (2019)
157. The Music Man (2019)
158. The Vampire Falls (Three Nights of the Vampire book 1) (2019)
159. The Other Ann (2019)
160. The Butcher's Husband and Other Stories (2019)
161. The Haunting of Lannister Hall (2019)
162. The Vampire Burns (Three Nights of the Vampire book 2) (2019)
163. Days 195 to 202 (Mass Extinction Event book 9) (2019)
164. Escape From Hotel Necro (2019)
165. The Vampire Rises (Three Nights of the Vampire book 3) (2019)
166. Ten Chimes to Midnight: A Collection of Ghost Stories (2019)
167. The Strangler's Daughter (2019)
168. The Beast on the Tracks (2019)
169. The Haunting of the King's Head (2019)
170. I Married a Serial Killer (2019)
171. Your Inhuman Heart (2020)
172. Days 203 to 210 (Mass Extinction Event book 10) (2020)
173. The Ghosts of David Brook (2020)
174. Days 349 to 356 (Mass Extinction Event book 11) (2020)

175. The Horror at Criven Farm (2020)
176. Mary (2020)
177. The Middlewych Experiment (Chaos Gear Annie book 1) (2020)
178. Days 357 to 364 (Mass Extinction Event book 12) (2020)
179. Day 365: The Final Day (Mass Extinction Event book 13) (2020)
180. The Haunting of Hathaway House (2020)
181. Don't Let the Devil Know Your Name (2020)
182. The Legend of Rinth (2020)
183. The Ghost of Old Coal House (2020)
184. The Root (2020)
185. I'm Not a Zombie (2020)
186. The Ghost of Annie Close (2020)
187. The Disappearance of Lonnie James (2020)
188. The Curse of the Langfords (2020)
189. The Haunting of Nelson Street (The Ghosts of Crowford 1) (2020)
190. Strange Little Horrors and Other Stories (2020)
191. The House Where She Died (2020)
192. The Revenge of the Mercy Belle (The Ghosts of Crowford 2) (2020)
193. The Ghost of Crowford School (The Ghosts of Crowford book 3) (2020)
194. The Haunting of Hardlocke House (2020)
195. The Cemetery Ghost (2020)
196. You Should Have Seen Her (2020)
197. The Portrait of Sister Elsa (The Ghosts of Crowford book 4) (2021)
198. The House on Fisher Street (2021)
199. The Haunting of the Crowford Hoy (The Ghosts of Crowford 5) (2021)
200. Trill (2021)
201. The Horror of the Crowford Empire (The Ghosts of Crowford 6) (2021)
202. Out There (The Ted Armitage Trilogy book 1) (2021)
203. The Nightmare of Crowford Hospital (The Ghosts of Crowford 7) (2021)
204. Twist Valley (The Ted Armitage Trilogy book 2) (2021)
205. The Great Beyond (The Ted Armitage Trilogy book 3) (2021)
206. The Haunting of Edward House (2021)
207. The Curse of the Crowford Grand (The Ghosts of Crowford 8) (2021)
208. How to Make a Ghost (2021)
209. The Ghosts of Crossley Manor (The Ghosts of Crowford 9) (2021)
210. The Haunting of Matthew Thorne (2021)
211. The Siege of Crowford Castle (The Ghosts of Crowford 10) (2021)
212. Daisy: The Complete Series (2021)
213. Bait (Bait book 1) (2021)
214. Origin (Bait book 2) (2021)
215. Heretic (Bait book 3) (2021)
216. Anna's Sister (2021)
217. The Haunting of Quist House (The Rose Files 1) (2021)
218. The Haunting of Crowford Station (The Ghosts of Crowford 11) (2022)

219. The Curse of Rosie Stone (2022)
220. The First Order (The Chronicles of Sister June book 1) (2022)
221. The Second Veil (The Chronicles of Sister June book 2) (2022)
222. The Graves of Crowford Rise (The Ghosts of Crowford 12) (2022)
223. Dead Man: The Resurrection of Morton Kane (2022)
224. The Third Beast (The Chronicles of Sister June book 3) (2022)
225. The Legend of the Crossley Stag (The Ghosts of Crowford 13) (2022)
226. One Star (2022)
227. The Ghost in Room 119 (2022)
228. The Fourth Shadow (The Chronicles of Sister June book 4) (2022)
229. The Soldier Without a Past (Dead Souls book 14) (2022)
230. The Ghosts of Marsh House (2022)
231. Wax: The Complete Series (2022)
232. The Phantom of Crowford Theatre (The Ghosts of Crowford 14) (2022)
233. The Haunting of Hurst House (Mercy Willow book 1) (2022)
234. Blood Rains Down From the Sky (The Deal Trilogy book 3) (2022)
235. The Spirit on Sidle Street (Mercy Willow book 2) (2022)
236. The Ghost of Gower Grange (Mercy Willow book 3) (2022)
237. The Curse of Clute Cottage (Mercy Willow book 4) (2022)
238. The Haunting of Anna Jenkins (Mercy Willow book 5) (2023)
239. The Death of Mercy Willow (Mercy Willow book 6) (2023)
240. Angel (2023)
241. The Eyes of Maddy Park (2023)
242. If You Didn't Like Me Then, You Probably Won't Like Me Now (2023)
243. The Terror of Torfork Tower (Mercy Willow 7) (2023)
244. The Phantom of Payne Priory (Mercy Willow 8) (2023)
245. The Devil on Davis Drive (Mercy Willow 9) (2023)
246. The Haunting of the Ghost of Tom Bell (Mercy Willow 10) (2023)
247. The Other Ghost of Gower Grange (Mercy Willow 11) (2023)
248. The Haunting of Olive Atkins (Mercy Willow 12) (2023)
249. The End of Marcy Willow (Mercy Willow 13) (2023)
250. The Last Haunted House on Mars and Other Stories (2023)
251. 1689 (The Haunting of Hadlow House 1) (2023)
252. 1722 (The Haunting of Hadlow House 2) (2023)
253. 1775 (The Haunting of Hadlow House 3) (2023)
254. The Terror of Crowford Carnival (The Ghosts of Crowford 15) (2023)
255. 1800 (The Haunting of Hadlow House 4) (2023)
256. 1837 (The Haunting of Hadlow House 5) (2023)
257. 1885 (The Haunting of Hadlow House 6) (2023)
258. 1901 (The Haunting of Hadlow House 7) (2023)
259. 1918 (The Haunting of Hadlow House 8) (2023)
260. The Secret of Adam Grey (The Ghosts of Crowford 16) (2023)
261. 1926 (The Haunting of Hadlow House 9) (2023)
262. 1939 (The Haunting of Hadlow House 10) (2023)

263. The Fifth Tomb (The Chronicles of Sister June 5) (2023)
264. 1966 (The Haunting of Hadlow House 11) (2023)
265. 1999 (The Haunting of Hadlow House 12) (2023)
266. The Hauntings of Mia Rush (2023)

AMY CROSS

For more information, visit:

www.amycross.com

Printed in Great Britain
by Amazon